THE OTHER
SHOE

By Mary McMullen

THE OTHER
SHOE

MARY McMULLEN

DOUBLEDAY & COMPANY, INC.
GARDEN CITY, NEW YORK

All of the characters in this book
are fictitious, and any resemblance
to actual persons, living or dead,
is purely coincidental.

To the man from Maryland

THE OTHER
SHOE

ONE

Answering an unexpected and unwelcome ring, at after ten o'clock at night, Justin Channon opened his door to the crash of the future.

His converted loft apartment was in a neighborhood where unannounced callers at any hour were to be regarded with suspicion. But the eyehole in the door had showed, pushing the figure to a distorted optical distance, a person appearing quite harmless, and yes—recognizable.

"Well," he said, pleasant but puzzled, "come in, Clare."

There was something about the way she moved, head high, shoulders straight and slightly back, that suggested she was facing into or up to something difficult. Her dress was at variance with the brave posture, a dress contrived of chiffon handkerchiefs, floating about her arms and breasts and knees, the color a seductive moonlit green.

In the center of the room, she turned and said, "Sorry to burst in on you like this. I did call, twice, but the line was busy. I was down this way for an opening and I thought I might as well—" She stopped herself, her eyes roving the room, a look of listening on her face. "I'm out of touch, is there a Mrs. Channon, or . . . ?"

"No. At the moment there are just the two of us here. Sit down and I'll get you a drink. Or, come along with me."

He hadn't remembered her as projecting a kind of nervous uncertainty. But then he hadn't seen her for years. Obviously she needed warmth and reassurance. Justin had a natural supply of both.

"Scotch, gin, what? Whose opening? Ferrault's? Between us, awful, I thought. By the way, as we aren't blood relatives but are connections"—he bent and gave her a light, friendly kiss on her temple—"it's nice to see you."

Her face flooded with color. "Oh, God," she said, "false pretences—a little scotch, please."

He poured the generous drink he thought was called for and added a brief dash of water. To keep her company, he mixed a gin and tonic for himself.

As if to cover the sudden raw words, she tilted back her head, looking upward, and said, "This kitchen is like a great whitewashed barn. I'd expect to see swallows nesting somewhere in a ceiling corner—does the word loft have anything to do with lofty? Did you remodel it, or did you find it this way? And the living room must be forty feet long."

He hadn't remembered her as a great producer of chatter, either.

"I did it. While we're in here, have you had any dinner?"

"Crackers with that fake caviar that the dye drips off." A gesture of her hand lightly refused any other sustenance.

"But did you come down here alone?"

"Yes, alone, why not alone?"

She looked to him like a woman who never need be alone, without a man at her side, except by choice. A little over medium height, with that independent supple carriage. Cornblond hair worn straight, side-parted. Wide sweet mouth, expressive eyes of a memorable summer-sea blue, and now, in July, an unexpected fling of freckles across her high cheekbones and over the bridge of her fine straight nose. She had seemed to him long ago a shining girl. The light had been put out.

They took their drinks into the living room and went to a corner where two couches right-angled. But she didn't sit down. She put her drink on the table and began wandering the room, which had no decorating scheme whatever but was full of interesting things.

She touched the head of a stuffed owl, tapped the glass of a little round barometer from France, paused before a Durer etching. Now she was studying titles in the floor-to-ceiling bookshelves, and he saw a reflection in the tall triple-mirror screen near the door to the kitchen: the graceful, green ghost. And himself, distant in shadows, sitting upright, interested, intent, on the paisley print of the couch. For one odd moment, it seemed to him that the reflection had always been there and would always remain there, as though painted on.

To what, he wondered, watching her steadily, do I owe the honor of this visit?

Now she was moving to his drawing board by one of the tall windows. Beside it, facing the room, was his typewriter on its table.

"I looked into one of your books once. I thought it was delightful. I suppose you do well with them?"

Justin was a writer and illustrator of children's books, the best known of which were his *Don't Tell Anybody* series. She stood looking down at a drawing thumbtacked to the board. "Is this for another *Don't Tell Anybody?*"

"Yes. D. T. A. about the Dithering Widgeon. And I do do well with them, within limits. Are you still painting?" He was beginning to feel uncomfortable. There was something a little unreal in this polite social exchange between, now, near-strangers. "Did someone say you show, in Paris?"

"Yes, once a year, but it's at a friend's gallery, so that makes it less impressive."

"Why Paris?" He found his glass empty and considered

refilling it. The tension in the room was growing, spreading to the farthest corners.

"I live there roughly half the year, the other half in . . ." Was there a flicker of hesitation? "Maryland."

She came over and sat down, picked up her drink and tasted it. "Oh, to hell with it. I came here to ask you about something. I'd thought about it ten times and this was the eleventh time. And then seeing you after years and years, seeing who and what you probably are, I mean—I thought again that it's ridiculous, mad, and was wondering how to get gracefully out of here, and fast."

"Whatever it is, say it—so there won't be a twelfth time to worry you." He leaned encouragingly toward her.

She took a folded paper from her little chain-handled bag. "Please don't be angry. If you only knew how I . . ."

He reached out a hand. "Give it here."

Plain white bond paper. The writing on it large and sprawly, in dark blue. "July 1, 1980. I suppose you think you got away with it and it's all forgotten. But it isn't forgotten and least of all by you. Could that be considered enough punishment for what you did? I say no." The one-word signature trailed off untidily at its final letters.

It could have been "Justice." It read equally well, or unwell, as "Justin."

He looked up and saw her eyes on him, the blue now an almost burning color.

He took a fast leap over his first reaction of astonished rage that he could be thought to have composed and sent this horrid communication—in its inconclusiveness, its unspecified windup threat, giving the impression of a nighttime whisper heard in a bad dream rather than an accusing daylight shout.

"Where's the envelope this came in?"

"I threw it away before I read the note. Automatic gesture."

"Do you remember the postmark?"

"I went back to the wastebasket and looked. Hagerstown."

He took an unopened Consolidated Edison bill from the

table and on the back of it wrote "Justin Channon, 14 Michael's Alley, New York." He gave her this sample. "I've omitted the zip code as it's cursive writing you're interested in and not numerals."

She looked at the strong, stylish, spiky hand. "I told you," her voice ashamed, low, "that it was ridiculous. Now on to my next sentence, to get out of here fast. I am sorry, Justin."

"No, wait, there are things I don't understand at all. Why not just crumple it up? You were found innocent, the book's closed."

"I was acquitted. Which is not at all the same thing as being found innocent. The first three or four weeks after the trial, I got letters like this by the dozens, from all over—one, as a matter of fact, from Johannesburg. But then the world apparently decided to turn its attention to other matters."

He found himself at a curious loss to take a firm position, help clear her air for her. The murder had happened the week after his wife had died. Through the shock and daze of grief, the distant crime on a peaceful Maryland farm lacked reality. He was able to give it no ear, no eye, no thread of his attention.

It struck him suddenly that all he knew about what had happened at Parish Landing was family hearsay, an amalgam of loyalties and partisanship, fascinated speculation and secret doubt. In a state of near collapse after Cornelia's death, he had been unable for weeks even to read a newspaper.

He pulled himself back to the present, to some shadowy pain he felt coming at him from the woman two feet away.

"And they never did find out, or have an idea about, who did it? I'm sorry to sound so blank, but sometimes these things land up in small paragraphs on page four or five after the big splash on the front page."

"No. They never did." She said this to the air in front of her, not to him.

It never occurred to him to question her genuine innocence.

"And after all the thunder and lightning, and after? what,

four years, when you're more or less back to normal—okay, some people will always think you were the one, to hell with them"—he picked up the folded paper, wanting to tear it across—"this arrives."

"Yes, in a nutshell." She gave him a surprised and grateful look. "The date is the exact anniversary, by the way."

Justin had a kind and tender heart. He didn't know whether it was sympathy, or a faint new guilt at having been so uninvolved himself in a tragedy in his own family, that made him want to put his arms around her, and comfort her, and tell her to forget it, because, really, everything was all right.

In any case, he wasn't at all sure that everything was all right. Some bent mind, simmering hatred, looking for an outlet, no matter how mistakenly chosen its victim.

"Could that be considered enough punishment? . . . I say no."

"Well." She started to get up and he took her hand and gently pulled her back down again.

"I'm sorry that I was away on another planet when it happened," he said.

"Yes, I know, your wife drowned—died—and I didn't even send a note or flowers or—"

"We were both on other planets. But to make up for it on my part, I want you to tell me."

"Tell you what?"

"Everything, dear," said Justin.

TWO

That summer, Clare had committed herself to three months with her Aunt Lelia, at the farm in Parish Landing, Maryland.

"I don't want you to feel *obligated*," Lelia had said in her soft leisurely voice. "But I've worn poor Cass down to her bone-ends and a kind, *rich* friend of hers wishes to take her to Europe. Of course, she'll end up carrying shawls and timing pills, but it will be in Paris or Barcelona, not in poky old Parish Landing."

Some of it he got—to augment his whole-minded listening—from swiftly interrupting questions.

("But why would you want to know about that, Justin?" "I do, though.")

Some of it reading between her lines, and reading her eyes. Some from his own freshly surfacing recollections of a week he had spent at Parish Landing, in summer, when he was twenty-seven.

Clare was obligated. Her father had died when she was an infant. Lelia and her husband, Robert Channon, had taken in the shattered young widow, Lelia's sister Eleanor Herne, and

her ten-month-old child, until Eleanor was able to find her
feet and earn a living and set up in a modest way for herself,
in Hagerstown. She had studied interior design before her
marriage and soon got commissions from friends. "Would you
do over the library? It's all tat and tack the way it is." "I have
an idea for a little garden house I'd like, just a sitting room
and bar and terrace by the lotus lake. Will you make it nice
and pretty?" Then friends of friends, captivated by Eleanor's
taste, came through with larger commissions.

But Eleanor was a poor manager, and extravagant, and
never seemed to have any money. Lelia had plenty of money,
no children, and when Clare turned seventeen, no husband.
Robert had died of a heart attack on the golf course of the
Parish Landing Country Club. There was no money in the
Herne till for further education after high school graduation.
"That child's talent can't be let go to waste," said Lelia, and
sent Clare to the Moore College of Art in Philadelphia.
"Young as she is," she assured Eleanor, "nobody can come to
any harm in *Philadelphia*."

When Clare was in her third year at Moore, a battered car
fresh from a hash party darted out of a side road, broadside
into Eleanor's car, and killed her. The driver and his six pas-
sengers, by some wry miracle, suffered only minor injuries.

"You must consider me," Lelia said to Clare after the funeral, "your surrogate mother. That is, insofar as I am *able*."

Because by that time Lelia had become an invalid. "Someone not under obligation," Clare summed up to Justin, "might
say that she was a spoiled beauty, getting on in age, and that
this was the shortest route to steady attention."

The cause of her indisposition was not clear. "The doctors
can't seem to agree," Lelia said. "I've been through five in the
past two years. Modern medicine to me is a disgrace." On her
good days, she got about slowly and gracefully with the help
of a silver-headed ebony cane. On her bad days, she occupied
her expensive pink-cushioned wheelchair, a perfect marvel of
engineering. On her worst days, she lay on her bed in her

darkened room and the house hushed itself to whispers and tiptoeing.

Her unpaid attendant was an indigent old friend, Cassandra Tucker, who came, at first with gratitude, to stay in the rambling house with its gardens and orchards.

When Clare arrived in June to spell Cass, Lelia said, "What a relief to have your face to look at. Poor Cass has such a sad sour way of looking *put*-upon."

Clare, at the softly commanding request for her company, had arranged a three-months' leave of absence from Happenstance House, where she had an agreeable well-paid job designing fabrics, china, and crystal. "Lord knows how many more summers the good God will send me," Lelia said, involving two members of the Trinity in her fate.

Her niece was not particularly surprised to find a good deal of her time on order. She had half-hoped that she could take a long plunge into her painting, not the weekend forays, but hours, days. The farm offered, in its one hundred acres and its vistas of tilted lilting meadows and plunging valleys, mistsmoked in the mornings, an itchily tempting place for the watercolorist. It was a farm only by recollection. The fowl and livestock had long since vanished, the once-ploughed fields drifted back to their knee-deep green, where white daisies grew, and pink and white clover, black-eyed susans and Indian paintbrush and Queen Anne's lace.

But Lelia liked to be read to—"My poor eyes get so tired"— and disliked lunching and dining alone. "I'm well enough today to take a little hobble about the garden. Come along with me and we'll take some sun." "I'm told there is the most wonderful sale of antiques in Braddock Heights. Let's run over in the car, shall we?"

Early mornings were Clare's best times. Lelia didn't get up until ten and, after her Earl Grey tea and thin toast, spent half an hour doing her face and hair.

If you got up at seven, and swallowed a fast cup of instant coffee, you had at least three and a half lovely hours.

About once a week, Lelia allowed herself a tantrum. Railing at her condition—a stricken woman, old, lonely, in pain, a bore. (She was not that old, but in her middle sixties.) She would refuse all food and drink, except for an occasional tiny brandy; she would pass from complaints into hysteria, have to be wheeled to her bedroom, and hovered over until the sobbing trailed off and stopped.

"Was it all an act?" Justin asked.

"I don't know. If you think you're ill and in pain, and getting worse, and may lose the use of your legs—who's to say you aren't? The old question, the body working on the mind or the other way around. But it did put her in center stage. And she did need that. Always the day after, a long session with the doctor."

"I suppose, considering her worldly goods, the doctor was willing to give her devoted attention?"

"To say the least."

Doctor Shoale had followed Doctor Ennis, who, when his patience finally snapped, told Lelia the best cure for what ailed her was to walk a mile every day, rain or shine. Without her cane.

Clare gathered that the new man had taken over in early April. Her first, and later unchanging, reaction to him was, I do not love thee, Dr. Shoale. He was a tall, thin man in his early fifties, who, she was sure, assumed his solemn lugubrious air just before he got out of his car at the house. He had a carefully tended black beard and sleek black hair brushed close to his narrow head. His skin was pale. He always wore formal dark clothing, a white shirt, and a subdued tie. "He looks like a Goddamned undertaker," Bryn had said.

"Bryn?" Justin, who had been lounging, sat up straight. "I remember Bryn—Hughes, was it?"

"Yes." A skipping-over syllable.

During that long-ago summertime week, it was clear to him that she and Bryn were a pair, and he found that they had been so since they were respectively ten and thirteen, when Bryn's family moved into the big brick house which was neighbor to the Channon farm. Clare spent her summers at the farm, in a far happier time when handsome Robert was alive, and Lelia was in health and spirits, and weekends the house overflowed with company.

She hadn't after all married Bryn. Well, people didn't always marry their first loves. She had looked, though, so wholly his. And vice versa. She her shining eighteen, he twenty-one.

But, he thought, a murder in the family can tear patterns to pieces.

Lelia was, on that Wednesday, several days late for her tantrum. When Clare brought her mail up at ten-fifteen she was sitting at her dressing table, a second cup of tea at hand. Her fingertips fluttered as she patted cream under her eyes.

"Eve of Rome. Costs the earth, but it works," she said. She looked fresh and pink this morning, younger and secretly pleased with herself. "You ought to start using it soon, Clare. You look a bit strained about the eyes. I suppose you're missing your lover?"

"Yes, I am, but he burns up the phone lines, as you know, and he may drive down with Meg if he can get away."

Lelia started on her throat with a cream that smelled of eucalyptus. "It's a mistake to sweep *upward*, it must always be down, down, lightly but firmly. Why people your age don't marry earlier is beyond me. *I* wouldn't have cared to take the risk of someone else snatching him. New York is full of good-looking girls."

"Perhaps this autumn. He wanted to find his feet first." Through family connections, which Bryn was blithe about using, he had just entered as a junior partner the prestige-laden Wall Street law firm of Starbuck, Dacre, and Prynne.

"Will you get me out my ruffled white? Doctor Shoale, dear man, ought to be here about eleven. I've never had anyone take such good care of me. I swear I'm beginning to feel better." Gazing at herself in the mirror, she amended, "A wee bit better, that is."

Clare resisted the temptation of telling her about Dr. Shoale at the Angels' Arms in Sharpsburg, twenty miles away. She had gone there last Saturday evening with Toby Tucker, Cass's pleasant nephew. Shoale, the undertaker-dark and solemn man, had been in a booth where, by a fortuitous arrangement of mirrors, she could see him but he couldn't see her.

Another man entirely, scarlet linen sports shirt, lean white duck pants, windblown dark hair falling casually over his forehead. Talking and laughing and busily drinking. His companion was a very young blonde with waistlength hair. Their manner with each other suggested physical intimacy. All right, people did relax off duty, and clothing could work amazing changes. But the contrast here was almost a visual insult to her aunt.

She could well imagine his—would it be amusement?—when he dressed the body of the other Dr. Shoale, and put on his face, to pay a visit to the farm.

With startlingly accurate timing, Lelia said to her mirror, "Such a fine man. So serious, devoted to his work. So dignified. Thank heavens a few of us care about maintaining standards in these tacky days." She dipped a swansdown puff into her face powder. "He told me that as a very young man he was torn between the ministry and medicine. He'd been most interested to hear about Grandpapa's lovely sermons and, of course, people did come from miles around to hear your great grandfather, Clare."

Clare found herself studying her aunt objectively. Lelia would be close to fifteen years older than Shoale. Midriff thickened from lack of exercise, but the rest of her still slender. Long face haughtily boned but softened and warmed, when she was in a good mood, by the large brilliant hazel eyes. Cosseted transparent skin, the lines on it as delicate as rose-leaf markings. Fine silky gray hair waving up and back from her brow and temples, attended to at home each week by Miss Ellie from the Salon de Beauté in Parish Landing.

Her first thought was, It's none of your business, don't interfere. But that could be looked at another way: even if you care about people—turn your back smartly and let them go down any particular and possibly disastrous chute. Don't put a hand out to stop the slide.

Perhaps it was personal prejudice on her part. But it wouldn't hurt to ask, here and there, a few questions about Dr. Shoale. Especially as it seemed clear to her that he deliberately encouraged her aunt in cherishing her illness. To say the least, unprofessional of him.

"Let me take care of you, my poor fragile darling, for the rest of your life—"

There wasn't, it turned out, time to ask a few questions.

Lelia touched the stopper of her perfume bottle to her earlobes and inner wrists, took off her pink bathrobe and put on her ruffled white. She scanned the room. Checking, Clare thought, her stageset.

"The chaise, I think. The fresh air from the window will do me good. Will you get me my blue mohair blanket from the bottom drawer? And you might do up the bed. Edna's probably busy with her ironing."

Lelia went to the window and leaned out, a new morning act for her. "Mmmmm. The roses, lovely. One more thing, will you put in a call to Ben Willett at the bank? The Market's having such peculiar ups and downs. He and I should put our heads together over the books and see how our finances look. Tell him tomorrow will suit."

To see how much dowry she could bring to the good doctor? Her complacent smile suggested that Clare was right.

Dr. Shoale arrived promptly at eleven. "Don't bother, I know my way," he said to Clare, and after putting in the call

to the bank she went off into the side garden. She sat on the
end of a lawn chair and tried to capture in watercolor the
breeze-trembling spangle of color and light before her. Time
flashed by; but when she heard his car engine start up, she
saw it was after twelve, and Lelia would want her company
for lunch.

The blue dutch door to the garden was open on top. She
heard Lelia's voice floating out of it. "Edna, I think lunch in
the garden. What smells so good? Salmon croquettes? Oh,
how nice. And I think you might bring out two glasses of
sherry first."

Not only downstairs today, but outdoors, and a discreet
midday drink. A good sign or a very bad one.

Sipping her sherry, and still wearing her white robe—after
all, she *was* an invalid although showing herself bright and
brave today, said the robe—she smiled on a bed of primroses.

"I have something amazing and astonishing to tell you,
Clare child. And I hope you'll think, delightful."

Oh *no*. Clare waited tensely. Perhaps, though, the doctor
had discovered a dramatic improvement in her health?

Savoring her niece's suspense, Lelia reached out and broke
off a pink-spotted white lily, sniffed it, and tucked the stem
through her top buttonhole.

"I'm to be married. *Married.*" She looked as dazzled and
sounded as dreamy as a young girl. "To, you guess who."

Clare now said it out loud. "Oh no!"

Ice and steel entered Lelia's soft voice. "*What do you
mean, oh no?*"

"But he's—you've only known him for three months or so—"

Lelia hurled her sherry glass to the slate-paved center of
the garden. Her voice rose rapidly. "And he's younger than I
am, you're saying. And he may be a fortune hunter, you're
saying. It is of course absolutely impossible and out of the
question that any man should want to marry poor sick old
Lelia for *herself*—" Her face was scarlet and her mouth and
cheeks began to shake.

"Lelia, please, for God's sake, quiet down—" Beyond Lelia's head, she saw Edna's startled face peering over the dutch door.

Lelia tried to get up and fell back in her chair. "Go!" she screamed. "Leave my house! You ungrateful girl—how you could dare—in a moment of the greatest happiness that's come to me in years—I won't have your death's-head around ruining it, ruining everything—yes, *go*."

Tears poured down the contorted cheeks. Clare moved to put an arm about her shoulder. Lelia picked up the silver-headed cane by her chair and struck out wildly with it. It hit Clare on the side of the neck. She fell down on one knee, feeling shock, pain, and a wet trickling. The summer day dizzied and darkened a little before her eyes.

"Good God almighty." Edna, a blurred Edna, came out and helped Lelia stand upright. Looking down at Clare she said, "Oh, ick. Blood." And then, "I don't know, Mrs. Channon, I think you'd be better off upstairs. Here, take my arm."

Clare listened to the rage of weeping until a door closed on it. She got to her feet and stood watching an Imperial butterfly quivering in blue beauty on the rim of her sherry glass.

Now what?

She couldn't in conscience obey the furious command, pack her bag right now and leave her aunt stranded. There might be, as after other tantrums, soft mournful apologies: "You must forgive this poor wretched soul, it's just that I was in pain and everything was suddenly too much for me . . ."

If there weren't apologies, if Lelia was really determined to get rid of her death's-head presence, the skeleton at her feast, something would have to be arranged.

In the meantime, a surface must be smoothed over the destroyed sunny July day.

Meg arrived in her car at three. She had broken the trip from New York to pay an overnight visit to her aunt in Hagerstown.

"You remember Meg, or do you?" Clare asked. "So long ago—"

"Yes," Justin said. "I remember Meg."

Poor kid, he had thought at the time.

Clare's close friend since early childhood, he gathered. "They're like sisters," Lelia said. "I love to see them together. The fair and the dark."

But it was unfortunate when friends as nearly linked as sisters loved the same young man. Bryn Hughes, a golden-colored match for Clare, thick spilling honey-dun hair, eyes of a darker blue than hers, merry and outgoing. A demon for exercise, tennis, bicycling, swimming.

"Justin, why don't you squire Meg?" Lelia requested. "Threesomes are awkward."

"It's perfectly clear that she looks on me as an elderly uncle," said twenty-seven-year-old Justin. "And I can't play tennis and never learned to swim. Un-American, isn't it? But I'll try."

Meg Revere was staying at the farm for a month. She had brought along the new car given her by her aunt for her eighteenth birthday, a pale blue Plymouth convertible. "Let's," she would say, "go somewhere in the *car*." She wasn't good at tennis, either, and was a timid swimmer, left behind near the shore while Clare and Bryn stroked swiftly far out into the shining blue of Parish Lake.

Perhaps, Justin thought, the two were so bound up in each other they didn't notice. Or maybe, unless you were a little in love yourself, as he was at the time, it wouldn't make itself so achingly clear to this bystander. Just the bumbles and blushes not unusual in a shy young girl, casual observers might think. And then Meg, too, had known Bryn, been friends with Bryn, from the very start.

As far as looks went, she needn't have lacked her own tennis partners and swimming companions. She was a slight but sturdy girl, soft in manner, with a heart-shaped face, dark curly hair, and large soft dark eyes. She had a delicate charm, modest but slowly and surely felt; a wood-violet quality to her. Why did she choose to expose herself to pain? For a whole month? Because, Justin answered himself, she loves him and she can't stay away from him.

Pain and persistence had, however, been rewarded. Three years back, while he was browsing through the Sunday *Times*, he came upon an account of the wedding of Margaret Revere and Bryn Hughes. A small, quiet wedding from the sound of it, no mention of attendants; at St. Thomas's, Fifth Avenue, New York.

Well, for a partner at Starbuck, Dacre, and Prynne, where else but St. Thomas's? Justin had thought at the time. He wondered a little about Clare and then guessed that probably from her point of view it wouldn't work, the two of them, in Bryn's professional world.

("Exxon is coming to dinner tomorrow, Clare."
"It will be quite a thrill to sit down with someone who was put on trial for murder.")

"I gave her two pills, I hope they were the right ones," Edna reported to Clare fifteen minutes after Lelia's weeping exit. "I've never seen her in such a state." There was a look of avid interest on her face. "What was it all about again?"

Edna Coats came five days a week to clean, tidy, wash and iron, and cook. She was reputed to be the illegitimate child of Judge Homer Dacre, a man much respected in Maryland. She left each evening to a tumbledown cottage overflowing with brothers and sisters of ages from three to thirty. Her large, fat, blond mother kept chickens and was in a small way of business. "Eggs and bags of chicken shit," Edna said scornfully. "Big deal. Me, I'd rather bake bread and scrub floors. At least the surroundings are okay." A short, thick, rosy girl with loose wavy ginger-colored hair, a snub nose, a good deal of insouciance, and (Lelia said behind her back) the Dacre eyes, mysterious and milk-blue.

Clare thought she had probably heard the whole thing and knew perfectly well what it was all about, but wanted the pleasure of a rehash.

"A mood," Clare said. She was rinsing out her bloodstained white linen shirt in the sink in the lavatory off the kitchen. The bandaging had been awkward, there at the base of her neck. The cut wasn't deep but bled busily while she washed it out and dabbed on Merthiolate.

"That's right," Edna said in mock approval. "Don't talk about the family with the help." Now as always she made no attempt to conceal her open dislike of Clare.

"Pay no attention," Lelia would say airily. "Jealousy, I suppose, and she's never rude to me, so rise above it."

Clare rose above it sufficiently to keep to herself the fact that Edna was by way of being a pilferer. A scarf, a bottle of perfume, a lipstick, a pair of pantyhose harvested to date from her bedroom. Oh, well.

Meg's arrival was a great comfort. Meg could be told everything, and promptly was. "If you feel a state of war hanging over this house," Clare said, "you are not imagining it."

"But you poor thing," Meg said. "There goes your money."

"What money?" Clare asked.

"Oh dear, I didn't know it was hush-hush—Aunt Fan told me, I can't remember when."

No one later believed that Clare hadn't known she was Lelia's heir. Not lock, stock, and barrel; there was a gift of furniture to a relative here, a modest annual income to another one there, a generous decking of the family tree with her jewelry. But the money, the land holdings, the farm, and the great brick house on Potomac Street in Hagerstown, were to go to Clare. Robert Channon having been one of six brothers, there were flocks of nieces and nephews and their mates and offspring. But Clare was the only niece of her blood.

"There were reams and reams written about it—about that

day and evening and night. And morning. You *must* have read some of it?"

Justin had not, but didn't want to go into explanations. "I'd rather hear it as it seemed to you."

"When the smoke clears, Meg, you can go up and say hello. And take her pulse, emotionally speaking."

But the smoke didn't clear. Lelia remained incommunicado, as far as the household went, in her room. Once, coming to listen nervously at the door—would the tears start again, was she asleep or just lying silently there?—Clare heard her talking to, she assumed, Dr. Shoale. "I'm in such a state of distress about *everything*, could you possibly . . . ? Oh. Oh no, of course you can't skip that. Tomorrow then, as early as you can make it after ten. Will you give some thought to some nice woman—not a registered but perhaps a practical nurse—who could do duty here for a while? Even great happiness, in this state of mine, tires me out. To say nothing of unhappiness."

Oh, God, Clare thought, feeling knee-deep in guilt. Thirteen impulsive words from her had been responsible for this wreckage. Why hadn't she said instead, How nice, how marvelous.

If medical care and attention were a major consideration in your life, it would be marvelous indeed, looked at objectively, to have in the same man your dear husband and your treasured physician. The only one of them who had showed himself grave, serious, deeply concerned about your condition.

For Meg's sake, she tried to make the evening as pleasant as possible. A cocktail in the slanting sunlight at the round white table in the side garden, lobster salad and a cold cucumber mousse she'd made the day before, demitasses. Questions about Meg's current life and her job, the answers to which she was almost too distressed to hear.

Meg was a stylist with a television film studio, Eyeways. It was a busy, adventurous, well-paid job, and she loved it. And was amusing about it.

Ending a story about trying to get a straw pannier filled with American Beauty roses onto a struggling, kicking donkey, she said, "Clare, you were supposed to laugh—do stop looking so sad. It will blow over, one way or another."

"Sorry. She's been good to me."

"Too bad Bryn couldn't make it." Voice light, as she nibbled a piece of Brie and picked up a slice of pear. "He'd have yanked you out of your melancholies. Let's walk down the lane and back—one mile, thirty-two calories strolled off."

Never let the sun go down on your anger, Clare's grandmother Herne used to say. Well, she wasn't angry but Lelia obviously still was. She and Meg read their books until eleven. On her way to bed, she stopped and knocked lightly on Lelia's door. "May I come in and say goodnight?"

Silence answered her, the silence of capsule-induced deep sleep, or rage uncooled.

"My bedroom was in the ell. Probably selfish of me, but I deliberately chose it when I got there in June because it was well along the hall, and down two steps, and up one, and then some more hall between the two of us. I thought she might drop into the habit of wanting to be read to at some midnight hour, or feeling a yen for hot milk or cocoa. I thought spoiling her wasn't a good idea."

"And," added Justin, "you might be eccentric enough to enjoy a decent night's sleep. Unlike other people."

She had waked at six to the dewed perfection of the summer morning, and to the weight of her guilt about Lelia like a stone on her chest. Too early to go and try to mend fences. But no, not too early. Lelia could always go back to sleep again. Because, Clare explained to herself, I cannot stand this one moment longer.

She knocked first, and again got no answer. She turned the knob and found to her surprise the door was unlocked. She went in, and stopped two feet from the doorway.

The big bed was roiled, sheets and summer blanket in an explosion of folds. Lelia lay facing the window, her body position awkward, one arm flung out behind her. There was something pale beige trailing over her shoulder and disappearing under a toss of sheet. As if to emphasize her total motionlessness, the white ruffled organdy curtain lifted in the morning breeze, floating forward. The yellow climber, burdened with bloom, half-lifted one rose over the top of the sill before the moving air let it drop back.

The room breathed death, and roses.

Was it before or after she forced herself to take one step, another, and then another, that she screamed? She couldn't later remember. It was an indecency to look at Lelia's face, to catch her unaware—the open blood-suffused eyes, the *tongue*— With an instinctive swift motion, she pulled the sheet over Lelia's head to give her a private hiding place. But not before she saw what had done this to her aunt: a pair of pantyhose.

On coming in, she had closed the door behind her. Now it burst open. Meg said, "Clare, what—?" and then seeing and reading the shape of the sheet, the covered head, herself screamed.

"No, don't look at her." Had she whispered it or said it aloud? Her ears were ringing.

Meg put out a hand to her. "Go away, go outside, sit down on the floor, put your head between your knees. I'll . . . see about a pulse, or heartbeat."

Clare obeyed, and experienced a brief drift into hazed gray, but not blackness, which might have been a matter of minutes or seconds. Through the haze she saw Meg's pink pajama legs going past at a run, and heard the sound of her bare feet on the stairs.

Meg called the police and went to the kitchen, where she made instant coffee and found brandy to pour in it. Coming back up, to a Clare now sitting silently on the top step of the stairway, she handed her a cup and said, "Darling, take it to your room and get dressed while you drink it. The police will probably be here in no time. I think your white nightgown is hardly . . . And I'll do the same thing."

But, Clare discovered herself thinking blankly, as she again obeyed, there were only the three of us in the house. Meg, and I, and Lelia. She took off her nightgown in her room and stood naked, shivering suddenly from head to toe. Well. Get dressed.

Reaching into the closet, her aimless fingers first touched a geranium-red linen dress. No, not a dress of that color, not today, not this morning.

She gave Justin a faint smile. "What I should have put on," she said, "was a suit of armor."

THREE

"If I'd been the district attorney, I wouldn't have had the gall to bring a case against you," Justin said. "On the evidence, I mean, or lack of it."

"Wouldn't you? That final quarrel—which was more or less one-sided, but how could I prove that? My great glaring white neck bandage, where I'd been hit by her cane. To say nothing of the loss of the Channon chattels to Doctor William Shoale."

The prosecution even made a point of her leave of absence from her job. "I suggest to you, members of the jury, that this young woman was informed, or had heard rumors, that Mrs. Channon's relationship with her physician was moving above and beyond the doctor-patient involvement. Who takes three *months* off from a perfectly good job at which the accused is reported to be well paid and highly regarded, with a salary of eighteen thousand dollars a year? She drops everything, packs her suitcase, arrives to stand guard."

In Shoale, she had a deadly enemy. Bad enough, the mere fact that he was a doctor. The court, while given as a body to complaining about the cost of medical care, and to regarding

medicine as a sure road to riches, still had a deep, holy awe
for the profession: the doctor as father, life-saver, God. If
your doctor could be wrong, all could be lost.

He was cool and quiet on the stand, showed no overt grief
or desire for revenge. "During that last telephone call, she
told me that for the fifth or sixth time she had asked her niece
to leave her house, that she found her presence distressing.
She called her"—a faint lift of one brow, a shadowed attempt
at a smile—"Miss Pinkerton. Referring I suppose to the leg-
endary detective agency."

"But obviously someone came into the house during the
night and killed her," Justin said. "You didn't, and I can't see
Meg—or not the Meg I knew for a little while."

"Obvious to you and to me. But, for a start, Meg's room
was right across the hall from Lelia's. And she didn't hear
anything. Anything at all."

Both the prosecution and the defense worked hard, for opposite reasons, on Meg's night. Was she a heavy or a light
sleeper as a general rule? Had she taken aspirin, or any kind
of sleeping medicine? Had she heard, repeat, anything at all,
even an innocent kind of sound, which when thought about
might open up the possibility of an intruder, however silent
the intruder was trying to be?

She was, Meg said confusedly, neither a heavy nor light
but, she supposed, a normal sleeper. She hadn't taken aspirin
or other medicine. She had waked at sometime after two and
heard a night bird but then fell back asleep.

The time of Lelia Channon's death had been medically cal-
culated as between two and three in the morning.

"I'm going to make something up," Meg said fiercely to
Clare before the trial began. "Say I heard the downstairs door
open and close—or a car in the driveway—or something—"

"No, don't," Clare said. "You're a wretched liar and they'll trip you up and catch you out. Which will only make things look worse for me. Reading between your lines, *you* think—in their interpretation—that I'm guilty and so are inventing any wild thing to get me off the hook."

"How was Meg, on the stand?" Justin asked.

The question puzzled Clare. "I think . . . just the way I'd be if the roles were reversed. Terribly distressed, voice shaking occasionally. Color coming and going, but mostly deadly pale."

"Oh," said Justin.

The house was secured in the normal way in that low-crime countryside. Front, side, and back doors locked, eight or nine windows open downstairs and up, screened, the screens all latched. The intruder, the night visitor, the murderer offered by the defense, left no convenient footprints on the drive or in the soft grass. No helpful thread of cloth caught in anything to be scientifically tabbed and traced later. No tossed-away cigarette butt. No evidence whatever of his or her existence.

The subject of keys was brought up and dropped, no use to either side. In a house two hundred years old, a house full of comings and goings, there would be a multitude of keys at large. And anyone with any knowledge of the house and its ways would know that extra keys were kept in the antique ironstone tureen on the hall table, along with a mysterious collection of buttons, nails, and screws, the leash of a dog long dead, and a rolled-up extension cord.

The pantyhose, too, was neither here nor there. It was a moderate-priced, nationally distributed brand, sold at both the Parish Landing drugstore and variety store. Clare said, yes, she occasionally shopped at both; but it was clear to all that so did almost everybody else in this little town of three thousand people.

The act itself, with this somehow indecent strangling device —could Clare, who had after all come down to *take care* of her aunt (heavy emphasis on these words) inform the court as

to what, if any, sleeping medicine or tranquilizer or potion
Mrs. Channon had taken that night, before retiring? Which
might have made her unaware of the sound of her killer,
approaching? No, she couldn't. Could she explain why she
couldn't? "But that's all been gone into, the quarrel." "I'd like
to hear your own version of it anyway." The defense instantly
objected to the word version. Word stricken from the record.
"Your own description, then."

Clare privately thought, but didn't say, that her aunt, when
she was in one of her moods, was apt to overdose herself at
night with her sleeping capsules, taking three instead of two,
as a sort of reckless revenge against everything and everyone
—including herself. She would probably have been deep, deep
down in drugged sleep when the pantyhose was slipped
around her neck. By the time she was aware enough to cry
out, there mightn't have been any breath or throat muscle
movement to cry out with.

"Did—leaving me out—the family rally round your flag?"
"Yes, the house was full of them, and I was allowed visits."
"Bryn?" Justin's voice was casual.
"No. He'd been sent to Paris, something to do with the
Rothschilds, something complicated, a stay of six weeks or so.
He cabled and said he was coming back even though it might
mean his job and I said no."
"Meg, of course, on hand?"
"They were wildly busy at her studio but she had to come
down to testify, and wanted to be of any help to me she
could. The poor thing shuttled back and forth at all hours.
She was there when the jury went out."

The trial lasted six days. It drew a large crowd of specta-
tors. Courtroom sketches of the principals in pastel, oil chalks,
and watercolor appeared on CBS, NBC, and ABC news. None
of your sordid mindless violence here, inflicted by nobody
people on other nobody people. Both the Hernes and the

Channons, particularly the Channons, were families of distinction and accomplishment. And an attractive young woman with straight sleek corn-blond hair—ghastly thrilling thought to think that those capable-looking, lightly browned hands had yanked the legs of the pantyhose tighter, tighter.

The jury was out five hours, the length of time, of course, a bad sign.

When the foreman delivered their verdict, his voice was dragging with reluctance. He said that the accused was found not guilty.

The guilt passed in a shadowy and inconclusive fashion to: a person or persons unknown.

"One of my fan letters said that if I'd been black and poor I'd be serving a life sentence or sizzling in the electric chair," Clare said. "Probably quite accurate."

To stretch his legs, Justin walked the length of the room and back. She had forgotten how he carried himself: how effortlessly straight, long legs with something of a dancer's grace in their easy stride.

"You've had four years to suffer for it and think about it," he said. "Who, do you think?"

"You'll understand that I don't like to toss names and conjectures about in a guessing game."

"Someone quietly sat back and let you go through hell. And changed your life for good and all one way or another, I suppose."

"You must remember," she said to him as she had said to herself hundreds of times, "that I dropped back into her life after seeing her only as an occasional visitor. She may have made an enemy, or a number of them. Gotten someone fired from a job, balked someone in a course or project that meant all the world to them. May have heard something scandalous, or disastrous, that she thought shouldn't be kept secret. And a dozen other possibilities. And then, every town, as you know, has its mentally odd souls. There could have been a blind mad resentment—her money, the farm, a servant to do for her. You may think *I'm* a bit mad, but I've tried as far as I'm able to pull a lid over the whole thing. It happened, it's over, and where do I go from there."

"No, I don't think you're even a little mad. That's what sanity is for, to stop you chewing on the unthinkable and the unbearable."

What she had said about the lid was only partly true. Every once in a while her lid rose to show the dark pit beneath. A look of startled recognition on a plane, on a train, at a party, and then the eyes turning devouring in their stare. At her last show in Paris, at the opening, a woman's voice in the buzzing crowd, ". . . we must have it. I not only love it, but look who did it. You remember about Clare *Herne?* That murder in Maryland? What a conversation piece we will own!"

For a short desperate time she had considered changing her name, altering her appearance, or both, but thought that identity loss on top of everything else could be a form of suicide. Goodbye, Clare, you're not you anymore, you're someone else from here on in.

A minor consideration: it could also be read as a confession of guilt. So would dumping the farm onto the real estate market. ("I'll never, never go near that place again.") So would refusing to touch the money Lelia had left her, and instead turning it over legally to be divided among the other heirs. ("I can't take that money, the deed of murder automatically cancels inheritance, so you can see that I . . .")

Mrs. Walter Channon did bring a suit against her, in an attempt to break the will. It was tried in chambers and got nowhere.

Clare kept the farm, which held lovely memories as well as frightful ones. She spent part of her year there, and part at her apartment in Paris. Paris had seemed a good idea, a clean sharp break, after the trial. And it was an ocean's distance from Bryn.

A little pattering sound brought her back to the present. Rain hitting the tall window behind the couch. She wondered how long she had been silent and thought how comfortable it was to be allowed silence by a man who was, after all, only a far memory. It was as though he had put a cushion under her head. Be quiet, relax. It's all right, you're safe.

Safe, how? And from what? She could not make herself take the mumbled threat in the note seriously. It was the writer, not the contents, that had brought her to her ridiculous—and come to think of it, insulting—mission to this address in SoHo. Why then the feeling, strange and warm and almost forgotten, of harbor?

"Where are you going from here, Clare?" Justin asked. It struck both of them in their separate ways as a somewhat metaphysical inquiry.

"To my hotel. The Brittany."

"And from there?"

She hesitated. "I'm of two minds. If it's going to start up all over again—Justice, whoever it is, pursuing me—Paris I think."

"I'd take the second turning," Justin advised. "The farm. Don't run away. This last time."

"*What* last time?"

"A feeling I have." It was a feeling, strong. Not a conscious and cohesive functioning of the intellect. "Right now, I suggest you go to bed. I'll try to make myself clearer over morning coffee."

"Oh, sorry—" She reached hastily for her bag. "I've been running on more or less forever—" Dismissed, blushing, polite about it.

"No, no, not at the Brittany. Here. I'd take you home in a cab but at this hour in the rain and in this neighborhood there won't be one. And you may be a brave soul but I am terrified of the subways after ten. There'd be a wait for a bus. In addition my raincoat would be much too big for you."

He was so matter-of-fact about it, kind and family friendly, that she thought it would be maidenly to put up arguments.

There was no problem, he explained. She could have the bed-room and he would take one of the couches. "I even have a new toothbrush still in its box. And a robe just back from the laundry on a hook on the bathroom door."

Efficient, fast, domestic, he went and got a pair of sheets and a pillow and made up the bed while she washed her face and brushed her teeth in the bathroom. She considered and discarded the idea of a hot bath. The running water might sound like some sort of sly female invitation. Here I am, alone, and naked now.

His bedroom was another barn, pleasantly underfurnished, the bed large, a reading lamp and a pile of books on the table beside it. She undressed swiftly and was in bed when there was a light knock at the door.

What now? And what else to say but "Come in"?

He had a glass in his hand. "A sleeping nightcap, milk with a little scotch in it. And may I have that note from your bag, in case you decide to tear it up and throw it away? Or in case —and promise me you won't—you wake up at some unlikely hour and think it's the better part of valor to flee this possible sex trap."

"Over there on the dresser, help yourself. And I won't be so ungrateful as to run away. And how can you be so kind?"

With a natural mild astonishment, "How could I not be, in your case? Goodnight, Clare." In the doorway, he turned. "There's an alarm clock on the second shelf on your table if you want to set it, but sleep as long as you like."

She drank her milk nightcap slowly and lay listening to the rain against the windows. She felt warm and drowsy and curiously at peace. Wrapped, in a way, in Justin, not merely his bed coverings. She slept.

Justin's publisher had been at him on and off for some time to write a book about his family. "With society more or less falling to pieces, people like reading about families. Your style is warm, you know, open. And you have, let's see, an actress, a surgeon with a maternity wing named after him, and, of course, your grandfather and the college he founded. *His* father, that daredevil minister. Your own father, of course, the eminent great lover and portrait painter. And wasn't there a murder somewhere in your family? You might like to skip that. But yes, do me a book on the Channons, dear fellow."

Justin had not been particularly tempted to embark on this chronicle. He foresaw, among other things, a rain of suits for libel and slander from the principals covered or from their descendants. And in a way it would be too much like looking endlessly in a mirror.

But for a matter of weeks now he had felt city-bound and restless. The *Widgeon* was almost finished; two or three full-time days would wrap it up as far as the writing went. He had completed the illustrations.

The project of the Channon biography, fake though it might be, would form a sort of visa: a reason, clear to all, for the asking of questions and the invasion of privacies.

He was imaginatively good at putting himself in other people's places and, lying awake early, put himself in Clare's now that she was real, flesh and blood, not just a name and face from the past.

How would it feel, to wear for a lifetime a dark invisible cloak of suspicion? "Did she or didn't she?" Had it prevented her marrying? "You'll be my wife, you'll have *my* name." "But I still have my own face."

You would be divided in two: the person you were and knew you were, and the person many still no doubt thought you to be, a woman of confidence and talent getting away with it beautifully. "You'd never believe it to look at her—so attractive the way she looks you right in the eye. But darling, be sure not to *cross* her."

It was entirely natural, if not flattering to the race, that people enjoyed believing the worst of their fellow humans; and in exact ratio to their appearance, abilities, and financial circumstances.

She could hardly expect the police to open up the case again on the strength of what would be to them simply a nutty note. Particularly as the note accused her all over again. She was a fly in amber, stuck forever, with only one non-solution offered.

Make the best of it, Clare.

There would inevitably be times when it would be impossible to avoid, on her part, reflecting back the suspicions of others. Why this weekend invitation? Why that sharp and sudden glance?—even though she must know she was a highly visible young woman. And could Justin Channon have sent that dreadful note?

Another *and*, which he hoped hadn't crossed her mind. Had he asked her to spend the night here on the assumption that she could afford no pride and had no reputation of any kind to lose? Briefly wanted her, and then contemptuously decided against it?

He could lie still no longer. He threw back the sheets, put on a robe, and went out to the kitchen to make coffee. The rain had stopped and had left behind not clear skies, but a dingy humid gray morning with a nameless reek in the air. The atmosphere—not unfamiliar in New York in July—was like the day after never.

From the door, Clare said, "A cup for me too, please. I believe you said you were going to make yourself clearer over morning coffee?"

She had dressed again in her floating green chiffon and in the dull kitchen daylight looked unreal, as if she had wandered onto the wrong stage.

"Slept well, I hope? Let me go wash my face and comb my hair for you."

They took their coffee into the living room. "Breakfast later, transfusion first." If he said so himself, his coffee was very good, hot and strong, made from beans freshly ground.

"Too many people, including me, Clare, have looked the other way too long. Would you mind if I turned my attention to what happened, and why? My next project, having to do with the family, a book, God help us, about the Channons, is going to take me to Parish Landing anyway. As well as other places." Sensible idea to let her think there was something in it for him.

"You're not planning to put me in a book?" she said with open horror.

"No, of course not, but who's to know that?"

"Are you saying then, that you are generous and maybe foolish enough to come to my aid—no matter how dead-end it may turn out to be?"

He would never forget the look in her eyes, the summer-sea blue eyes, a faraway dawning of a quietly buried hope.

"Yes," Justin said, and added a summing-up question which she found later to be one of his favorites. "Why not?"

FOUR

It wasn't easy to get hold of Meg Revere. She was now, it seemed, a very important person at Eyeways Studios, vice president and executive producer. Odd to think of quiet Meg, with her heart-shaped face and curly hair, wearing those ringing titles.

Her secretary, on the telephone, said she was tied up for, let's see, at least three hours, and then a casting session loomed; perhaps he might try again just before the session started, say at six o'clock?

What horrible hours the poor girl works, Justin thought. He had the luxury of handling his own time any way he liked, and except for the past few long, deadline days usually spent a maximum of five hours a day at his typewriter and drawing board. He was not party to the American belief in hard work for hard work's sake. Life, he said, is too short for that nonsense. But Meg must work because she wanted to. Surely the wife of a corporation lawyer wouldn't need the money.

He called again at six. Oh dear, Mrs. Hughes was still tied up—no, wait a moment, here she was. Justin, sitting in a pair of white shorts in his apartment, said mendaciously that he found himself in her part of town and could she join him for a

drink after her casting session? He'd suddenly been reminded
of her and thought it would be nice to see her again, he explained.

Money, success, and general rushing around seemed to have
changed her soft voice. Oh, and she was ten years older, too.
She said crisply, "Just let me look and see if anyone else has
nailed me—no, but it would have to be fast." A little as though
she were granting a favor and not accepting an invitation.
"Say eight o'clock at La Signora."

La Signora was on West Fifty-fifth Street just off Ninth Avenue. It must be good, or fashionable, Justin concluded, to
survive in such a location. He got there ten minutes early because, besides being prompt by a natural courtesy, he wanted
to see her entrance whole. An empty small corner table in the
candlelit bar faced the door. He chose it, and waited without
a great deal of patience for forty minutes.

There at last she was. Still slight and sturdy in build, but
everything else altered. The curls cut short and close to her
head in an Adonis crop. Face thinner, or maybe it was the immense smoked amber glasses. Expensive underplayed chic to
her clothes: a narrow bare-armed white linen dress with a
Persian silk scarf looped around the hips, white thong sandals,
an immense turquoise burlap bag probably by some status
designer slung by its strap over one shoulder. The very brown
summer skin of people who weekended in the Hamptons.

Yes, you're right, her entrance informed the watching occu-
pants of the bar. I am somebody.

She stood looking around for a moment, then saw him
standing up in his corner. She came over swiftly, stood on tip-
toe, and kissed him on the jaw. "Justin! What a sweet surprise," not troubling to lower her voice. "And darling, just as
beautiful as ever." What first crossed Justin's mind was "Pro-
duction by Meg Revere."

To the approaching waiter, she said in a self-service fashion, "Dry martini, please," and then to Justin, "Not done at

this hour but I haven't eaten yet. Must get there soon." Quick glance at her watch.

Take off your glasses, Justin said silently. I want to see who you are, whom you've become.

"I was surprised that you remembered me," he said, when her drink arrived and she took her first hungry sip.

"But why? How could anyone forget you? When I was a gangling lovesick idiot, you came on like the king of the world and took me dancing. With Clare and Bryn. You had on a double-vented cream-colored suit and a lavender gingham shirt from London. Here I was with a grown-up drop-dead man."

Why was she talking so fast, brightly, flatteringly? Or did she always talk that way now?

"Take off your glasses, Meg. I want to see if I remember you right, too."

She did, with what seemed like a touch of reluctance. He looked at and into her eyes.

But Meg, you are destroyed.

Why?

After a portion of a second, she blinked, public face back on, the eyes dark, clear, and brilliantly sparkling. She reached out for the glasses. "Those ghastly glaring lights in the studio—"

He hoped that his face hadn't been readable, his shock. Perhaps it had, because she gave a little laugh like a caw and said, "When you called, do you know what I thought? That you were looking for a job, were out of work or something and thought Eyeways could fit you in somewhere. Maybe even as an actor or model. We do both commercials and films, you may have heard. I came braced, as you can imagine. You have no idea how many people— I mean, it seemed so odd, after ten years, your popping up out of nowhere. And how or by whom were you suddenly reminded of me, by the way?"

"Clare. She was down in my part of town—SoHo—and dropped in to see me."

Meg, who had been about to take a second sip, put her glass down. Her eyes were well shielded but her small delicate mouth hardened. *"Wicked* Clare! Oh, sorry, unfortunate word choice—but to be here in New York and not let me know! I suppose she was on the wing, passing through to Paris?"

"Yes, she did say something about Paris." He didn't immediately understand his own evasiveness. "You don't, then, see each other very often?"

"No, separate paths and all that kind of thing. She avoids New York like the plague and we—Bryn and I—never seem to be able to get away anywhere for more than a weekend."

We. Investigate that. "I find it hard to keep track of whose wife is now married to whose husband. You're still married to Bryn?"

"Yes. Very, as they say, much so. He's in Belgium at the moment."

"And, children?"

"No." She drained her drink. "I can just manage another fast one."

Natural enough that the two, or the three, should avoid social contact. Clare had been in love with Bryn and he with her. Bryn was married to Meg.

Natural enough at first—but after all this time?

During the second drink, she asked what he did for a living. "Unless, darling, you're independently wealthy."

He told her and she said she must remember his books when their friends' children's birthdays came along. "Now I must run." They said goodbye, not goodnight, on the sidewalk in front of La Signora. There wasn't an, Now that we've met again we must pick up where we left off.

You wanted to have a drink with me, you've had a drink with me, and now we will go off, and back into our own lives.

But it was odd that she hadn't asked him what he was going to do with the rest of his evening. Hadn't, as might have been expected by an old acquaintance ("How could anyone forget you?"), taking the trouble to look her up and buy her a drink, suggested that he come along with her to wherever she was dining. Darling, one extra won't make any difference.

Not feeling inclined to sit down, order and consume a large expensive meal, he walked across town to P. J. Clarke's, where he had a drink at the bar while he waited ten minutes for a table. Over his hamburger and glass of Valpolicella, he went on thinking about Meg.

Perhaps it was the drive of ambition, and the work it entailed, which had wiped out the wood-violet girl and replaced her with the clanging young executive.

Perhaps the marriage wasn't happy, hadn't worked, or wasn't working now. Still hungry, he ordered a cup of chili and over it sketched out a plot of how the marriage might have come about.

Bryn rushing back from Paris when he had finished up his Rothschilds business, and wanting naturally to stand by Clare in the strongest possible, permanent way: as her husband. Clare refusing for the reasons which had presented themselves to him before. Refusing not once, but four times, nine. The three of them, close since early adolescence. The two of them, Bryn and Meg, with the tight warm bond of their love and concern for Clare growing tighter. How long after the trial had the marriage taken place? He wasn't sure, but he thought it was about a year.

Bryn finally giving up and turning to Meg, who, in a way, was part of Clare. Not the healthiest basis for a marriage.

If I can't have her, I'll have you. The next best thing?

Meg as she was now wasn't a woman to let a failing or failed marriage slip through her fingers. He could almost hear her saying, We'll work things out, Bryn, see if we don't. It's just a matter of applied intelligence.

He had been avoiding the little sting, or stab, which might have been totally accidental or innocent. "*Wicked* Clare! Oh, sorry, an unfortunate word choice—"

Why explain, why drop that in, when as she went on her choice of the accusatory adjective was perfectly clear?

A thought from nowhere flicked across his mind.

Wicked Meg.

Now where had that come from? It was one-sided and unfair, and, in a way, alarming. Because it underlined a feeling he had hardly been aware of, that he was of course on Clare's side, and committed.

FIVE

It would have been pleasant to think about staying at the farm, right on the scene, right at the core. But whereas films, magazines, and newspapers were fashionably permissive, many people—especially people in a little town—were not.

The Parish Landing Inn, as he remembered, was a bit dressy and a motel did not appeal. Why not, it suddenly occurred to him, kill two birds with one stone? Every few months his stepmother called him from Siderno, in Italy, where she and his father lived in a little stone villa on the Ionian Sea. At least once a year she could say, "I hope *somebody* visits poor Hannah now and then. The least you can do, Justin, is send her a present or a card for her birthday. Or both. I haven't got her street address but surely you can dig it up." Jenny was his father's third wife and very intrigued to be finally enmeshed in a large family, having been an only child of only-children parents.

His Aunt Hannah was the relict of his uncle Thomas Channon. She was unofficially known in the family as the Poor Soul. Her husband had excelled his five more successful brothers only in the consumption of drink. He had been, among other things, a majordomo at an undertaker's estab-

lishment, a Bible salesman, and a cataloguer of private librar-
ies. The second eldest of the brothers, he had died fourteen
years ago, leaving his wife a small annuity, the premiums
stubbornly paid for to Prudential come hell or high water.
Justin remembered him as a pink-and-white, soft-voiced man
of great sweetness.

He had no idea whether or not Hannah was a late sleeper
and waited until eleven in the morning to call her.

He had some things to attend to in her neighborhood, he
said, and might he stay at her house for a short time? She
lived in Channonville, three miles from Parish Landing. He
fully intended to pay for his accommodations but thought he
would save that arrangement until he got there.

"You'd be welcome," Hannah said. "I almost never see anyone. Of the family, that is."

He thought about her word "almost" as he packed his bag.
It would be a bad day in his own life if and when Hannah arrived to stay. In her own and her husband's family, and
among her friends and acquaintances, she performed the
function of a kind of deathwatch beetle. Anyone in the last
throes, or looking close to them, could count on Hannah's
turning up in her dusty black Volkswagen, to Help. However
extensive, expensive, and professional the care of the patient
was, there was no keeping Hannah away.

"Not really mad, but eccentric doesn't quite cover it," Justin's father had remarked on his last visit to attend the funeral
of his brother Ives. "Thank God she can't drive her Volkswagen to Italy."

Justin had dispatched his manuscript to his friend, typist,
and one-woman answering service, Jane Rand. In the note he
left for his cleaning woman, he wrote, "I'm off for a bit, I
don't know how long." He placed on the note money to cover
this Tuesday and next Tuesday, and took a one o'clock plane
to Washington. New York wasn't hard to leave behind, caught
in an immense pocket of hot, soiled gray air. Washington was
worse.

At the airport, he rented a green Volvo and drove the fifty-odd miles northwest to Channonville. It was a quiet little town bypassed by time, as though the decades had not seen it lying there in its soft hills. Orchard and dairy country mainly, three green and peaceful miles back from the C & O Canal. There was no industry, no rail service. The bus went through only twice a day.

Hannah Channon lived in a house on Ballard Lane, off Main Street. On approach, it looked more like a waving tall green mound than a house. It was a thin dark wooden structure surrounded on three sides by porches, over which grapevines had long ago been grown. They had thriven and interlocked and reached upward to the roof and chimney, and dropped thick curtains over the porch openings. The effect was at once romantic and neglected.

A house to be saved, Justin thought, for one of his books; indeed a place like something out of a tale. A good thing he had brought his camera along.

The green gloom enveloped him as he stood waiting at the door after he had rung the bell. It opened and a green-faced Hannah said, "Come in, Justin," and lifted a cheek to be kissed.

She was a little fat woman who moved with surprising speed on her still-slender legs. Her hair was dyed a lightless black, center-parted and bunned at the nape of her short thick neck. Her eyes were dark brown and had a way of darting and flickering around in their sockets, which had always reminded Justin of the rapid scuttle of cockroaches when kitchen lights were unexpectedly turned on at night. Her mouth was gloomy. She wore a mysterious shapeless brown garment, which must have been made by her own hands. The wide sleeves stopped at the elbows and showed her strong plump forearms.

"You are looking well." Soft voice, Louisiana, formal in diction. "Of course, I hear you are quite successful. Not overdoing I hope—how has your health been?"

"Marvelous," said Justin emphatically.

"Well, you must be tired after your long journey, anyone, however strong, would be. I've done out your room, come along on up." She was swift and agile, ahead of him on the stairway.

The room was large, its furniture and double wardrobes old and dark and heavy. There was a white cotton spread on the bed and a faded flowered rug on the floor. Over all floated an agreeable pattern of grapeleaf shadows and sunlight, gold and green; the effect a little dizzying at first as though the room itself was floating on water.

"Very nice," Justin said. "You won't mind if I wander around occasionally taking pictures here?"

"You are my guest," Hannah said. "Do as you please."

"Well, yes and no. They want"—what would they want?— "twenty-seven fifty a day at the motel up the street and I thought I'd rather you have it."

"Very well. I shall accept it with pleasure. After you've unpacked I have some wine for you, I make it myself. The bathroom's across the hall, only the one I'm afraid, although there is a lavatory in the cellar. I'll be on the front porch."

Her voice had been lowering as she approached the closed door. Opening it, she turned and said in a near-whisper, "If you'll remember to be as quiet as possible for the time being? I don't want to wake him."

"Wake whom?"

"Bryn," Hannah said. "Bryn Hughes. I fear he was not quite sober when he came. I feel he needs his rest," still in her *ssshhh* voice. "I told him the guest room was to be occupied by prearrangement. He's in the nursery. I don't know whether or not he means to stay." She silently disappeared.

Hannah and Tom had had no children; Justin assumed that the nursery meant a small room fit to deposit a small body in. He felt the tingle of shock to his finger ends.

When last heard of—yesterday—Bryn was in Belgium.

While he unpacked his bag he wondered if this was the

reason for the look in Meg's eyes of somebody lost and gone.
A love affair that had never ended, with Clare, powerfully
alive and steadily pursued. His wife's cool proud cover-up.
Bryn's in Belgium. In San Francisco. In New Orleans. But
could you, in his vice-presidential boardroom world, just dis-
appear at random, a week at a time? Hardly. It must be a
matter of the snatched few days. "I've got this damned virus.
I'm condemned to a short spell in bed."

His own rising unaccountable rage was a shock to him, too.
My God, wait, stop. The reason he was here was that he
thought that the wrong conclusions about Clare, about the
murder of Lelia, had been gleefully leaped on and clung to.
And here he was, blasting and condemning her, and Bryn, in
a matter of a few seconds. Taking for granted the wriggling
busy worm in the apple.

Bryn's parents might still be living in Parish Landing for all
he knew. But then why wasn't he in Parish Landing?

To hell with it, let the man wake up, give Bryn a decent
chance. Bryn and Clare. Perhaps if he had had a drink too
many, he'd thought it would be a good idea not to drive any
farther. Pull up at Hannah's and rest a bit.

There hadn't been any car in front of the house.

To hell with it.

Going down the stairs, he registered with his perceptive
nose the house smells. Dust, a stale hint of pork grease, a
breath of mold and mice, a whiff of carbolic; the combined
odor of pennies being pinched hard, if not of outright poverty.
He wondered if his father had remembered to send his annual
check to Hannah and decided to become a contributor himself.

He wondered if Hannah had inherited any money from
Lelia.

She was waiting for him in her wicker rocker on the porch.
There was a bottle of wine on the round wicker table. "Help
yourself, Justin, and I will take an inch or so to keep you company."

To his surprise it was good wine, the blue Concord grapes of course, but dry and delicate, pleasantly cool from the cellar. "To you," he said, lifting his glass. "I think at my advanced age I might drop the 'aunt.' Is that all right, Hannah?"

"Yes, do. How old *are* you, Justin? You always look, I don't know, the same age. Or rather you looked older when you were younger and you look younger now that you're older."

"Thirty-eight."

"While I'm being personal, may I ask what brings you here?"

Try it out. "I'm thinking of doing a book on the family and I thought I'd start at the source."

"How interesting. You do know that this whole town was Channon property? You do know it was a King's Grant? The first one—I've always been proud his name was Thomas, too—got here, I can't remember when, in the sixteen hundreds."

"I'll look it up in the library, I'm not sure myself." It sounded all right, the book project. It sounded innocent, and real.

It was very quiet on the porch. He smelled honeysuckle, near, and on the breeze hot tar, a road being mended not far away. There was a muted sound of cars on Main Street.

Hannah's train of thought, like her eyes, took a sudden skitter. "July is always a sad month for me. Poor Lelia. And that nice woman who finally gave in to her ulcers. Thomas died in July, right after the fireworks on the Fourth. And didn't your poor wife—was it off a sailboat? Or have I gotten her mixed up with the Ladley girl who also . . . ?"

"Not a sailboat," Justin said. "She was swimming, off Montauk Point on Long Island. She got caught by what they call a sea pussy, a streak of undertow, and was carried out a mile. She was a good swimmer but by the time a boat went to look for her, and spotted her fighting a wave eighty or ninety yards away, it was too late."

Cornelia had gone out to the Ryders' cottage in Montauk on a Friday. He was to join her on Saturday for the weekend. She wasn't there to join, in any way whatever. The body was never found.

"Oh dear, oh dear," Hannah sighed. "Just as I said, a sad month for all of us."

Motion was necessary. He put down his glass. "I think I'll give Clare Herne a ring if you'll excuse me a moment." The telephone was on the hall table, a directory hanging by a string from a nail on the table edge. Herne, Clare, 11 Rumsey Road, 898-0069. Six rings, seven. Don't hang up yet, she might be outside. At the fifteenth ring, he did hang up. He looked while he was at it at the H listings and found five Hugheses, but couldn't remember what Bryn's father's name was.

Discretion could be carried too far. Going back to the porch, he said, "About Bryn—do his family still spend summers here?" His air was one of mild interest.

"Oh no. She died—heart, poor thing, I was able to be helpful at the end—and he sold the place. I haven't seen him, Evan Hughes, since a little while after Lelia met her unfortunate fate." She sighed again. "I often think if I'd been there seeing to things for her she might still be alive. I offered a hundred times to look in, and give a hand, but it was odd, for some reason she wanted no part of me."

Justin didn't think it was odd at all. It was one thing to occupy yourself at enjoying ill health but quite another to see the deathwatch beetle ready to preside at your bedside.

Then Bryn was not here to see his parents. But he'd spent summers in Parish Landing since he was thirteen years old. He must have dozens of friends hereabouts.

On a visit then? Without Meg? "We never seem to be able to get away anywhere for more than a weekend."

Put that aside.

There was something he wanted to find out and the sooner the better.

"Lelia did leave me my great-grandfather's cuff links." An invention on his part; and his voice just barely questioning.

"She left me—oh . . . how grasping we sound, sitting here counting things on our fingertips." She abruptly turned money matters off and scuttled to a hasty new topic.

"This light becomes you, Justin." Her mouth turned small and sour. "But then it must be nice to be you. Some people are fortunate. Some are not."

She gazed at him in a drinking-in way. He had a classical face and head, speaking gray-blue eyes under emphatically hooked brows, and a Roman nose over a thoughtful mouth. Leisurely long body in the wicker chair, product of some comely ancestral sculptors from genes and genes back. He wore a brown-and-white striped seersucker suit with his usual air of freshly showered ease. There was about him, even in stillness, a graceful quiet authority; an inner harmony with himself.

He was calm under her inspection. It led her off onto another tack. "To think of Clare all alone in that big place—and it standing *empty* half the year! Justin, you haven't remarried, or if you have I have not been informed. Neither is she, you know. Wouldn't it be nice if you married each other?" She shook her head as at an impossibility. "Of course you hardly know her."

"What's going on here—matches being made among the vines?" inquired a voice from the other side of the screened front door.

SIX

They met as if it had been half an hour, and not a decade ago, since they had parted company.

"Well, for God's sake, large as life—Justin."

"Bryn!"

A swift handclasp. The bloodshot whites made Bryn's eyes look bluer. His hair was the same dun-blond, sleep-tossed and thick down over his forehead. He had evidently napped in his shirt and trousers. They were damply creased.

No, not destroyed like Meg, Justin registered immediately. Besides being a little drunk still, he looked unhappy and torn and wore an air of rakishness, or recklessness. But not gone. Yet.

The white square-toothed smile banished for a moment the impression of a man stricken down with an inner sadness. "I'm about to be hit with claustrophobia here on your nice blind leafy porch, Hannah. Justin, is that your car I see in front? Will you take me out and air me?" He bent and kissed Hannah's forehead. "You'll excuse us?"

"Yes indeed. I'm due up the road in half an hour. Poor Mrs. Whaley."

"Poor Mr. Hughes," added Bryn. "Give me two minutes to wash, Justin."

He was down again in under five minutes, fresh pink-and-white striped shirt, white shorts, leather sandals, skin gleaming with soap and water and hair smoothly brushed.

Leaving the porch, Justin said, "We'll feed ourselves, Hannah, when the times comes."

As they got into the car, Bryn said, "Then you're the house guest. I gathered in my vague state on arrival that there was one expected. What are you doing here?"

Justin told him about his book. Bryn, listening and not listening, said, "Well anyway, you're a godsend. There's no one to talk to, up there." With a sweeping gesture of his arm he disposed of the entire northeast. "Strangest thing, when I saw you—does everybody else think you're his brother or is it just me? You're too polite to say, Why are you bottling around Channonville instead of rushing home from abroad to wife and dictating machine? Well, you poor devil, I'm going to tell you what I'm doing here."

There was a dam-bursting feeling behind the words. But then, if you had to have a confidant, Justin thought, what better one than a stranger who belonged to the past, the sunny past, and who had no connection with wives or Wall Street.

"Which direction do you want to take your air in?"

"Just a meander, for the moment." Bryn fell silent. It was getting on for four o'clock. Their narrow road curved, climbed and fell between dry stone walls heaped with honeysuckle in white and yellow blossom. Beyond the walls were fields of rye, delicately blued and gold and green. Stands of immense trees, sycamore, maple, oak, pouring a midnight of shade gave the landscape the look of a superbly executed painting.

Seeming to take it for granted that Justin knew about his marriage to Meg, Bryn picked up his own immediate story without preamble.

"I'd resisted coming down here a thousand times. You may or may not believe it, but my last attempt was two years ago.

I haven't been near the place since. When you're in another country, you get a long scary view of that little scurrying dot across the ocean who thinks he's Bryn Hughes. You drink a lot, on business and on planes, and things either get very muddy or very clear, depending on how you look at them. I knew I had to make another Parish Landing run. I called her from the airport—"

"Clare?"

"Yes, of course Clare. I wasn't even sure she was in this country. I told her I was coming and she said please don't and I said, expect me in the afternoon. I had them wire ahead, from the plane, for the company jet. We landed about two and I got the one taxi to drive me out to the farm. There was no one there. The gate wasn't locked, and neither was the front door. It was as though she was saying, all right, come in, Bryn, except that I won't be here. Ever."

He ran a hand over his flushed face. "I wandered around. I went up to her bedroom and lay down for a while on her bed. I opened her closet door and sniffed at her clothes. Then I felt that something invisible was pushing me out of the house. I got a chill and my teeth started to chatter. Just so she'd know I'd been there I left her a note in the telephone prongs. A very simple note: 'I love you.' I left and walked to town and into the bar at the Inn, where I tried restoratives, a lot of them. I decided to give it one more day, she might have relented after going away like that, in her car—the car wasn't there. Suddenly I remembered that old witch Hannah and thought she might know where Clare would be likely to be on a summer afternoon. I took a cab to her house and half-fell up her front steps. Well, no food since early morning, in addition to— She took one beady look at me and conducted me to bed."

Justin had been twenty-three before he discovered what was physically meant by the phrase, the bowels of compassion. Now there was the near-painful turning-over feeling in his gut. Always vicarious, never compassion for oneself.

"What," he asked, "had you been going to do if she was there waiting for you?"

"At the least, make love to her. Or try. At the most, get her all back again. Tell her I'd divorce Meg. Marry her or live with her forever after or whatever she chose." He turned and gave Justin a long piercing look. "I hope I'm right about you. Spilling things this way. You wouldn't peach on me?" Word from early childhood. "But then you don't know Meg—or yes, you met her once down here."

Justin didn't want to go into his meeting with Meg. Too hard to explain, dismiss, in front of this man somehow and suddenly so close. Instead, he said, "As you haven't had any food, shall we stop? There's a place right up ahead."

Bryn said yes, all right. The King's Arms, three dining rooms full of new antiques, fresh flowers on the tables; a luncheon meeting place for garden club ladies. The hostess looked thoughtfully at Bryn's brown legs in his white shorts and led them to a table in the deserted bar. Bryn glanced at the menu, written in uncertain French, and lifted his blood-shot innocent eyes to the organdy-aproned waitress. "I'm just up, dear girl, I want breakfast. Bring me bacon and eggs, please, and huckleberry muffins. And a pot of coffee, not a cup."

"Yes, sir," said the obviously charmed girl. "And the other gentleman?"

"Would I lead you astray if I had a drink?" Justin asked Bryn.

"No. I'll stuff first, and join you later."

He fell hungrily on his food, and into silence again. His companion, who was good at silences, drank his scotch and water slowly. Should he be offering sound advice, urging Bryn back to his wife and his office? But surely after four years of being torn every which way, Bryn now knew his own mind. I want what I want and devil take the hindmost. The hindmost being Meg.

Bryn drank the last of his coffee, crumpled his napkin and

tossed it on the table, and called over to the bar, "Martini, please, double, dry."

"And what are your plans now, if any?"

"I'll try once more. She may have relented, as I said. She might have come back and thought, oh well, I could at least talk to him when he's come all this way. Will you drive me there, Justin?"

"No," Justin said. "I won't. I can listen and I can sympathize but I can't deliver the body."

Bryn gave him a sad white grin. "You won't in other words be my accomplice. A party to this scandalous arrangement or attempt at one. Yes, I see that. All right. I left my big bag in the bar at the Inn. You won't object to dropping me there? Stopping first at Hannah's for my other one?"

They left after he had his martini. Under the Inn portico, Bryn said, "I'll be in touch with you before I go. If I go. Even if you won't be an accomplice, you might wish me luck under your breath. And if no luck, I'd like to see you when you get back to New York. Often. Bye, mate."

He thought about calling Clare from the bar and then decided against it. She might melt away again; if she had ever come home from her wanderings. But forge ahead. You don't, Bryn told himself, let everything go after one quick unsuccessful foray.

Everything.

"Here's your trusty customer again," he said to the taxi man at his stand outside the Inn. "Eleven Rumsey Road."

"Channon's farm, you mean—we don't call that place to mind as a number."

It struck Meg as odd that Bryn wasn't home, at the apartment, when she called at a little after four from her room at the Villiers Hotel in New Orleans.

His normal procedure after a transatlantic flight was to collapse into bed for a long nap. There must, then, have been something pressing to see to at the office.

He wasn't at the office either. Ethel Adams, his secretary, said he'd sent a message to have the company plane meet him at Kennedy.

"And where was it to take him?"

"The message didn't say, Mrs. Hughes. Is there anything wrong? You sound—"

"You haven't a note of any immediate appointment of his out of town?"

"No, but something may have come up in Brussels."

"Look, Ethel, I must somehow get in touch with him, I'm in New Orleans and a terrific emergency has come up. Will you try to find out for me where the plane was taking him and call me back? Here's my number."

Ethel radioed the jet, now on its way to Maine to pick up two barrels of fresh-caught lobsters. She asked Danny Bloom, the pilot, where Mr. Hughes had been going, and had he gotten there? It was very important, she added. Danny gave her the destination reluctantly. And yes, he'd gotten there. "I hope I'm not getting Mr. Hughes in trouble," he said. He liked Bryn Hughes. "He might just have been playing hooky." "But it's his *wife* who wants him, Danny." "That's sort of what I meant," Danny said.

Glowing with her own efficiency, Ethel called the Villiers Hotel.

"He went to a place called Parish Landing, in Maryland, Mrs. Hughes."

"Oh, you are a love, Ethel, thanks so much."

"Glad to be able to help. And I hope whatever it is gets straightened out."

The gate was still unlocked. He didn't want the taxi driver sharing, with local curiosity, his possibly empty arrival. He paid him, got out, and walked slowly up the drive, putting off the moment when there might be nobody there.

The scent of roses floated by on the breeze. Orioles sang in the great maples to the left and right of the house and behind it. They created their own purple-shadowed twilight but through a trunk or branch here and there he saw the dazzling green-gold of the lifting meadows, long away from their own twilight. It was seven o'clock.

The front door opened under his hand. "Clare?" he called softly, and then shouted with all the power of his lungs, "*Clare!*" The vibrations of his voice loosened a few petals of the larkspur spires in a ginger jar on the table between the living room windows. The little blue flakes of petal drifted down to the blue and amber Izmir rug.

Had she come home at all, had she read his note? It was still there in the telephone prongs. He picked it up. Yes, she had been home. On the other side of the note she had written, "I'm sorry, Bryn. I've gotten over you."

It was a little over two miles back to town. He walked it, very fast. He went into the Inn, collected his bags, borrowed without charge a bedroom to change his clothes in, and checked the airline schedule in his billfold. Yes, he could make his plane if he drove fast enough. There was always the chance of being picked up for speeding on the main roads but he knew some timesaving cutoffs where he could really let go.

He had a final martini at the bar. He could neither taste nor feel it.

Hurry. Get away from here. Back to noise and bustle, people, crowds of them, back to urgent matters of law and finance to be dealt with, meetings and conferences to be attended, international decisions to be made with cool dispatch. He had forgotten how much easier it was in New York. You could fill your days, your life, jam it to the remotest corners, never stay still, never be alone to have to think.

There were no orioles, no petals falling to a madman's shout, no whispering of maple leaves at a window screen, to disturb and penetrate the steady roar.

He snatched a minute to call Justin. He felt a need to say goodbye to him. Hannah answered. Yes, Justin was there.

"I'm off. See you in New York."

"Then, no luck?" Not curious or probing. Kind.

"No." Christ, he'd better hang up, he felt as though he were going to burst into tears.

Something about the tone of his voice made Justin say, "Are you all right? Shouldn't you stay there overnight and get some sleep?"

"I'm all right. See you, Justin."

I've gotten over you I've gotten over you I've gotten—Hurry.

He all but ran to Dixon's Car Rental, two blocks up the street. Joe Dixon said, "Sorry, Mr. Hughes, all my cars are sewed up. Wedding party. But I have a phone message here for you, from a"—he winked—"Mr. Channon. D'you suppose it's a joke? You're to call him immediately."

"I called back but you'd left the Inn and I thought I might find you at Dixon's," Justin said. "I'll drive you down. Washington, is it?"

"But I can't possibly let you."

"Why not? My time is my own. And there's a girl I'd been thinking about seeing there anyway. I'll pick you up in ten minutes under the portico."

Death had not been kind to Justin. His mother, whom he adored, had died when he was eight. His only brother Gilbert had at nineteen, on the way home from a party, misjudged a curve and smashed his MG and his short life into a pine tree. His wife Cornelia had gone silently out to sea.

"I suppose, Justin," his Aunt Esther had said once, "that that's why you're such a preserver of life, if those are the right words."

He didn't think now that Bryn had overt suicide in mind. But he did think that he was in a mood to embrace with open arms the possibility of disaster. Guards savagely flung down, leaving him vulnerable to whatever dreadful thing might happen to him between here and Washington.

Bryn swore to himself and then accepted the step back from the edge of an unseen beckoning cliff.

The invented wedding party commandeering all Dixon's cars for rent, later cost Justin eighty-five dollars in, he suspected, mythical lost rentals. "And cheap at that," said Joe Dixon.

SEVEN

Hannah's bathroom had no shower and the tub water, luke-
warm, ran rusty for a while before clearing. After drawing
four inches of this unappealing blend, Justin was not tempted
to lounge about in his morning bath. There was a thinned-
down cake of Ivory soap in the dish and a sere gray-pink
washcloth over the tub edge which he left to itself. He reminded himself to buy soap and a sponge.

But he shouldn't be contemplating matters of personal sani-
tation; he should be thinking bright and early about his two
clients. One, whoever it was who had killed Lelia. And two,
because of course it couldn't be the same person, the writer of
that not very veiled threat. "Could that be considered enough
punishment? I say no." Was the punishment to be meted out
slowly, in the form of more notes, more mystery? Or was it to
strike physically, next month or next week or today?

The Hagerstown postmark didn't necessarily indicate a resi-
dent of that city. It was only forty miles from Parish Landing
and was the place where you went for serious shopping, or
hospital visiting, or expensive dental work, or partying, or visiting relatives. It was the lodestar for Cumberland Valley
towns in a circle of at least fifty miles on the compass points.

It would be a convenient anonymous place to post a letter from.

The note, on the other hand, might mean nothing more than a cry of mindless venom carried on the wind.

But it offered an opportunity to turn knobs, open doors; to get to know his cast of characters.

He dressed and went down to the kitchen, which smelled of sour mops. Hannah, light-footed, appeared beside him. "There's coffee keeping warm on the stove. Would you like a nice dish of hot oatmeal? It's been cooking for hours in the double boiler. So sustaining."

Hot oatmeal on a hot July morning lacked attraction but Justin assented gracefully, washing the thick mixture down with two cups of the coffee, which was unexpectedly good.

"Doctor Shoale still here I suppose?" he asked, eying a large clotted lump of oatmeal in the bottom of the bowl and bypassing it.

"Oh yes, he's built up quite a practice." She poured herself a cup of coffee and sat down at the table with him. She wore the same ample brown garment she had worn yesterday. "More or less everyone in town is a patient of his, now or eventually. Doctor Deere is quite elderly—eighty-two and semi-retired. And Doctor Seldon drinks. Or could it be drugs? You only go to Doctor Seldon when you can't get an appointment with Doctor Shoale. More oatmeal?"

"No, thank you. Delicious." Justin got up and carried his bowl to the sink.

"You are a nice thoughtful boy." Then with sudden alarm, "But Justin, do you need a *doctor?*"

"No—just idle curiosity. Is there anything I can pick up for you in the way of shopping? Although I don't know when I'll be back."

"Oh, that would be kind. It's hot for marketing." She got up and tore a little piece of paper off a brown paper bag standing on the counter, found a pencil in her pocket, and stood scribbling.

Her list read, "head of cabbage, fresh ham if cheap, packet of lg nails, hrdwr store." Her handwriting slanted backward and bore no resemblance to that of Clare's sinister correspondent. It sent him another, minor message: it might be advisable to dine out tonight.

"Off about your researches now?"

"Yes indeed," said Justin, and drove through the hazed, humid morning to the address he had looked up in the telephone book on his way out the door. Parish Landing Medical Center, announced the large sign on the circle of clipped lawn. Medical, dental, and X ray services housed in a new-looking low brick building. Dr. Shoale's offices occupied a good half of the long structure. Large waiting room which could have been anywhere in the United States, wall-to-wall dull gold and green carpeting, green vinyl chairs, sofas, and loveseats, a low table with a stack of magazines, a railed-off area to the left of the door containing two white-clad girls, desks, telephones, and shelves jammed with the folders of patients' records. And, inevitably, people waiting, six of them.

The girl at the front desk studied him in a leisurely way with her strange milky-blue eyes. Waving ginger hair, a rosiness to her—yes, Clare's description had been exact. Edna Coats. Graduated from cleaning help to doctor's aide.

"*You* look familiar," she said after her survey was completed. "Photographs, a painting? I don't know, but Channon one way or another." Her manner was breezy and—flirtatious wasn't the word, it was an open sexual waft she sent directly at him.

She hadn't liked Clare, possibly jealous of her. Shake her up, why not? "And you're Edna Coats."

She stared, then smiled. "I didn't know I was all that famous all the way to where you come from. Willett it is now, though. Mrs. Benjamin Willett. I only work for fun, get to see a lot of people. I don't need to, you know, my husband's with the bank, vice-president." She spoke not in a murmured confidential way but for all the room to listen to. Ma Coats' girl, having escaped the chickens and the children and the scrubbing of other people's floors, now Mrs. Banking Willett.

"I haven't an appointment," Justin began, "but—"

The phone rang and she picked it up. He watched her hand taking down a message on her pad. Upside down, he read, "Mrs. Stone has a head cold and won't be able to come in at 2:30." Not unpromising, the loose formation of the letters. But he'd have to have a closer look, and right side up.

She replaced the receiver. "This is your first visit, isn't it? You'll have to fill in this sheet"—giving him a mimeographed form—"but then you can go straight in."

He had no idea why she chose to jump him over the six people waiting, unless it was a small brandishing of authority and power. "Now see here," a woman near the desk began to protest. "Emergency," said Edna airily. "He don't look like an emergency," the woman grumbled. Justin had his form filled out and handed back when a door across the room opened and a man with a bandaged head came out. "Next!" called Edna briskly. "Mr. Justin Channon." She pressed a button and announced him over the intercom.

Dr. Shoale, in his own office, did himself well. Two fine Persian prayer rugs, a walnut French desk, handsome walnut and steel bookshelves, and a large and very good painting by an artist Justin didn't know, an abstraction emitting light and strength. Shoale sat at the desk busily writing, probably notes on the patient who had just exited. He raised his sleek dark head and gave Justin a quick but thoroughly assessing look. His skin was pale and suggested that it would be cold to the touch. He had a puritan's spare tight mouth in odd contrast to a heavy self-willed jaw.

"And what brings you here, Mr. Channon?"

Justin sat down in the chair facing the doctor. "I've dried up for the moment but I can't seem to stop sneezing. And I have this very severe headache, behind this eye, aspirin won't do a thing for it. Do you suppose it could be the honeysuckle? An allergy of some kind?"

"You look remarkably well for a man with a racking head-ache," Shoale said crisply. "Eyes clear as a bell. Where are you from, that honeysuckle would come as such a shock to your passages?"

"New York."

"But surely—considering the name—you must have had some contact on and off with the Maryland countryside? Do you always have these attacks when you come here?"

"No, but they say that your whole physical makeup changes, is it every seven years?"

"Well, one immediate remedy would be to go straight back to New York." Shoale's thin smile indicated that this was to be taken as a medical quip. "You could, of course, go through the whole scale of allergy tests—how long do you plan to be here?"

"I have no idea. Visiting around, you know."

He was aware of the narrowed dark eyes trying to read him. Then, with a gesture of impatience, Shoale drew his pre-scription pad toward him. Writing, he said, "This handles most of the common allergies. You'd better pick up a bottle right away—seeing the pain you say you're suffering. If it doesn't work, come back and we'll have to put you through the hoops."

Justin thanked him, put the prescription in his billfold, and went back to the waiting room. Edna wasn't at her desk. "Twenty dollars, Mr. Channon," the girl at the desk behind said, and got up to find a file on the shelves. The rail was nar-row and Justin bent to Edna's desk to write his check. First he flicked off the top sheet of the phone pad and pocketed it. Comparisons weren't immediately possible. The Clare letter was back at Hannah's, in his suitcase; a caution taken because he had been relieved in New York over the past three years of several billfolds.

There was a public telephone booth in front of the medical center. He dialed New York Information, got Bryn's number, and, in another minute, Bryn. "Just wanted to see if you made it all right," he said.

"Thanks, Justin, I did." Voice sounding tired and late-night hoarse. "Very kind of you to worry about me. I'm alone here— Meg's in New Orleans. They're shooting some trash or other— a series about a young whore in the French quarter who finds out she was kidnapped as a child and is of noble birth and . . . Anyway, be sure not to miss it if and when it survives its screenings." He must be lonely, or nervous, to rattle on so about something that bored him. A hesitation, and then, "You'll mind your tongue when you do get to see Meg, which you will? I did not go straight from Brussels to Parish Landing. Damn fool way to get to New York, I'd say. Let me know when you get back. Oh, one more thing. Did I dream it or was Hannah trying to pair you up with Clare, on the porch?"

"A fantasy," Justin said obliquely.

"Well, lay off, mate. In any case. Good luck with your literary endeavors."

Justin's next call was to Clare. He got no answer. Could she still be bent on evading Bryn?

Before leaving the booth, he decided to pursue the wordless invitation which had been sent at him in the waiting room. It was the other girl who answered. "Doctor Shoale's office, Prunella speaking, may I help you? . . . Yes, here she is, Mr. Channon."

Could Edna by any chance have lunch with him? There was a surprised "*oh*" from her and if a smile could be heard along a wire he was hearing one. Well no, she was sorry but it was her day to have lunch in, a sandwich at her desk, and Prunella's day to have lunch out. "Perhaps a drink on your way home?" pressed Justin, and got a swift yes. "My husband has the car, he took it to Atlanta, a banking convention. (Clear road for you, Mr. Channon.) My own's laid up. Prunella was going to drive me home." She would, she said, be ready and waiting at six o'clock.

He drove to the public library, an old, low white brick

house with an English garden in front. From the pleasant young woman at the desk, he asked for newspapers of his required dates, Baltimore, Hagerstown, and the Parish Landing *Courier.*

"You must be Mr. Channon," the librarian said. "It's nice to have a writer on the premises. Your aunt's been in and took out the *Penny-A-Bite* cookbook. Well, at the price of food I must read it myself." He feared more of her kind distracting chatter but she led him into what had obviously once been the kitchen of the house, with a big square scrubbed table in the center and a faint haunting of spices and yeast. After a short time she came back with an immense armload of newspapers, and delivered herself of only a little more chat.

"Your aunt said you were writing a new book. About the family. We have a lovely set of the Reverend Hall Channon's sermons. You'll be wanting to look at those I wouldn't wonder. Five volumes."

"Perhaps another day," Justin said. He got out a small notebook from his breast pocket and settled down to his hard steady homework. The Press point of view and that of the protagonists might differ sharply.

Not wanting to discourage himself with the sound of empty ringing, he drove to the farm at a little before noon. It was an oppressive day, the hidden sun sending thick heat through a low cloud cover. The trees were hazed in their own green breathing.

He turned in at the open gate between white-painted board fences. Meadowland deep in wildflowers to the left of the grassy earth drive, old orchards of apple, peach, and pear to its right. Then a tunnel formed by flanking maples opening at the other end to show a sloping lawn, only casually tended, blue here and there with butterfly bushes. The house in its trees and gardens was at the top of the slope. Not a grand house, and built onto at different times and by different tastes; but an agreeable one. Two-story fieldstone in front, a brick wing making the ell, a lacy wooden summerhouse with a cone-shaped green roof attached to the ell at right angles by a breezeway covered in purple clematis. There was a long walled fieldstone terrace across the front, with wide shallow steps frothed in cracks and corners with ground phlox, or as Maryland called it, cemetery moss.

He felt the sense of fragrant and old and settled peace about the scene. It looked like the sort of place where nothing not pleasant could ever happen. Especially—a word like a shock on the tongue—murder.

He left the car at the terrace steps and went up them and across to the screen door. There was movement in the shadowy hall and then Clare opened the door to him.

"Justin! How nice, come in."

For an illusory second she seemed more like light and music than flesh and bone. Or perhaps it was the pearly gleam of her white silk shirt, tucked into slender white pants. Or the sunlit-sea blue eyes.

"To celebrate your arrival, I'll fix us juleps, even though there isn't a horse race within fifty miles."

Like her house, she looked as if she had, not now or ever, anything to do with that darkest of syllables, death.

EIGHT

The house made it all much more real.

He stood in the broad center hall in a listening attitude. Two or three o'clock in the morning, the invader's feet going up those stairs to his left. The staircase was painted white, with a banister rail of slim round white pickets. Down its center was a worn hooked runner, a dim pattern of roses and tulips. The runner would help muffle the soft and carefully stealing ascent. But this was an old house. Surely a step here or there would utter the aged creaks of worn wood under stress.

"Justin?" Clare came out of the kitchen at the end of the hall to the right with two frosted pewter julep cups which sent up a green cool smell of mint. "Am I interrupting something?"

"I'd like to wander around for a minute or two, is that all right?"

"Yes. I'll be on the terrace." Nice of her, understanding, to let him try out his tendrils combing the air, alone.

He went slowly up the stairs as if he, too, were planning a desperate deed. He had thought all along that it had been a sudden-emergency killing. Who would choose of his own accord the listening silences of deep night? And a guest in the house, a third listener? But it simply had to be done, done immediately.

The fourth stair up let out a peculiar humming whine.

Hannah would be, what? about his weight, perhaps a little under it. He thought the time had come to loosen the strings of normal daily intelligence and let it fly and float like a kite in the wind. Hannah wasn't welcome here as a nursing aide but must, after all these years, know the house and its quirks.

On the seventh stair, there was a crisp loud *crackkk*.

Could you have memorized the tricky stairs and skipped them? Hard to handle in the dark, above the pounding of your heart and the holding of your breath.

Say you were Ben Willett, called to give an unexpected accounting of monetary affairs, so that a besotted woman might know to the last penny what her dowry was: what treasure she would be able to bring to her dear doctor. Would you have practiced the stairclimb earlier?

No. Because you hadn't known until the morning of the day before that you absolutely had to be here, at this dark hour, in this sleeping house.

If you were Edna, you would know all about the steps, having cleaned up and down them a hundred times. But leaving out the betraying terrifying noises, how would you know a door would not be flung open, a voice demanding, "Who's there? Who is it?" And a light turned on, and you caught flat-footed if not yet redhanded.

Well, that wasn't too hard to figure out. You would have a backup statement ready, just in case. Whoever you were.

I was passing and I thought I saw reddish smoke at the back of the house. I thought I'd better wake someone up.

I saw a car shoot out of your driveway, two drugged-looking louts in it, and thought there might have been trouble, harm done here to someone.

The door key, not a problem. "Oh, didn't you know the front door was unlocked?" Even normally careful people sometimes forget to lock their doors at night, or mistakenly thought someone else had remembered to lock them.

You would obviously have to know which room was Lelia's. It wouldn't do to open the wrong door. Oh sorry, wrong victim, pardon me.

On his long-ago visit, he had once gone up to Lelia and Robert's bedroom to fetch her book from her bedside table. "Would you, dear? I feel so lazy sitting here under my tree."

A front room, to his left. He opened the door. In the newspaper accounts, it had been referred to with relish as the Murder Room. The door hinges uttered no sounds. It was probably his imagination, but there was an embalmed look to the great brass bed with its antique white crochet spread, to the pale blue taffeta chaise longue by the window, to the ruffled white organdy curtains. The room was clean and dusted. Did anyone ever sleep here? Guests, perhaps? Would anyone want to sleep here?

The door directly across the hall opened into the bedroom where Meg had been sleeping. He went in. A fresh and cheerful place, no pall of death hanging here. Yellow and white chintz at the windows and covering the bed, a round yellow rug on old floorboards painted a soft dull orange. No sounds to be heard, except an oriole on a maple branch outside lighting the moment with music. No sounds had been heard here that night either. Except a bird, Meg had testified, some night bird.

Well, she had had the two-day drive from New York. He himself, city-trained, was able to sleep soundly through the commotion of ambulances and police and fire sirens. And perhaps it had been so swift and skillful, the killing—Lelia making it easier, deeply drugged as she might have been—that there had been no sounds to hear. Or sounds loud enough, frightening enough, to wake a healthy young sleeper.

The closet door was on the other side of the bed. He went over and opened it. So real was the sense of living again that silent disastrous night that he almost expected to see Meg's clothes on their hangers. But the big closet was empty, smelling a little of summer damp.

He pulled himself back to the present and went down to join Clare. She was propped against the terrace wall as if she was too restless to sit down and too uncertain to stand with her usual arrowy straightness.

Bryn, probably, but—"Have you been getting any more of your fan mail?" he asked.

"No. When I got back here, I did find myself brooding about my waiting punishment. I thought, I'll get into the car and start the engine and it will blow up. Or there will be cyanide in this sugar I am rolling my strawberries in. Or, it might be wise not to go to sleep tonight, with just a screen between me and Justice. Needless to say, that way madness lies. So let's both, please, forget it."

It seemed unlike her, this near-rude abruptness. Was it guilt, about Bryn? Was she saying, Please go away, I don't, after all, want you prying and poking into the hidden corners of my life?

As though reading the silent question, she said, "It's a very small world down here. You may very well have run across Bryn."

He thought it would be unwise to start off with secrets and little gulfs between them, especially as he had no intention whatever of allowing himself to be dismissed and sent home.

"Yes, I had a drink with him yesterday afternoon and later I drove him to Washington to get his plane for New York."

"That was an unusually kind deed. For a stranger." Again, he ventured inside her head. *What were you doing, pumping him? Seeing how much about us you could find out?*

"He wasn't able to get a car to rent. And my schedule is loose to say the least." Go away, Bryn, from the air around us, and stay away. You have nothing whatever to do with the reason for my being here.

He took a deliberate long pull at his julep and changed the subject with a crash. "I will on and off be asking you unrelated and perhaps silly questions, but please be patient. What did Hannah get from Lelia?"

"An annuity of five thousand a year."

"What did Tom's annuity amount to?"

"Twenty-five hundred, I think. Last year, to round figures out for you, a grateful woman she'd been taking care of left her fifty thousand dollars."

He was startled. "But she gives every evidence of living on the edge of poverty."

"She's by way of being a bit of a miser—I suppose all those years with poor Uncle Tom terrified her of ever being broke again."

"I gather the police weren't very much interested in Hannah."

"Among other things, the police chief's mother was one of her patients. And, anyway, people don't connect tending the sick with dealing out violent death."

"She said she was asleep in her bed when it happened. Channonville is only a little over two miles from Parish Landing," Justin mused. "No need to go bustling around in the night hours in her car. She could have walked. She's very fast on her feet. I suppose I'm wearying you—you've probably been over all this in your head a hundred times."

"No, you're not wearying me, and I'm grateful for a fresh eye. But what would I do, face her and say, 'Now then, Hannah, out with it. A signed confession would simplify things.' Or, the same statement to anybody else who wished to agree that my wild and wandering suspicions about them were correct."

He could almost see why she had settled for a flawed life.

But his position was different: he was accused of nothing and could not be regarded as desperately attempting to shift the burden of blame. And besides, he was writing a book. No doubt most of the town knew it by now. A highly visible stranger with a permit to seek out fresh material for this particular chapter of the Channon family story. Intrusive people, these writers. Nothing sacred, if it looked good in print. Or profitable.

"Did Edna get anything?"

"Not a cent."

"You don't suppose she'd been lifting things from Lelia and Lelia threatened to turn her over to the police—unlike you with your charitable silence?"

"No, Lelia would have broadcast it from the housetops and fired her immediately."

Or so you think, Justin amended mentally.

"Did you—afterward—fire her or did she leave?"

"She left, after three days of cooking for and cleaning up after the relatives. I imagine she only did that out of curiosity and a sort of pleasure in all the . . . bloody drama."

"And Willett? His accounts must have been gone over to see that everything was kosher? All clean and ready for Lelia's overnight summons?"

The heat was getting to him. He felt an odd weariness, as if it was he, instead of she, who had been all through this before, years of it, dreams about it, long endless tunnels, mazes, of questions and possibilities to lose himself in. He took off his seersucker jacket and looked with disappointment into his empty julep cup.

Clare smiled at him. "Poor Justin, thirsty work. I'll get you another."

Coming back, she said, "Her lawyers in Hagerstown took over, of course, after she died. I suppose naturally they would have taken a close look at the state of things."

"Did she handle investments and so on through them?"

"Mostly through Ben Willett, I think. She liked having a bank vice-president at her beck and call."

Her lawyers wouldn't know, then, whether their client had told her bank v.p. to sell A and buy B or C; or what verbal instructions he might have acted under.

He changed the context but not the subject. "Edna Coats

and a local bigwig banker? How did that come about, the marriage?"

"Even bankers can be overcome by storms of unruly passion," Clare said, looking amused. "I think he'd lusted after her for years, but he was very much under the thumb of his mother. Lived with her, of course. She wouldn't hear of the match, daughter of the town jezebel. It's beside the point, perhaps, but she looked—his mother—like Calvin Coolidge. Anyway, she died and two months later he married Edna. That was between two and three years ago."

Justin thought it would be very interesting to meet a passionate banker. He looked forward to it.

"Strange that he doesn't keep her in a bank vault during the day," he said. "She's going to have a drink with me this evening."

"During which you will hear additional unattractive things about me, to add to your collection." Collection? Bryn again? Of course.

"I didn't come here to find out unattractive things about you, Clare." She looked away from his blue-gray gaze, open and kind, and dropped her eyes.

A car came out of the green tunnel and drew up behind the Volvo. The far door slammed and then Meg came running up the steps, bringing with her an air of sudden distant thunder in the hot heavy day. She stopped on the top step and stared at the two.

"I was on my way back from New Orleans," she began breathlessly, "and I thought— What the *hell* are you doing here, Justin?"

Clare straightened lazily from her leaning position against the terrace wall. She went over to Justin, and stood in front of him. She tilted her head back so that her cheek rested in the hollow between his jaw and shoulder and put her arms backward around him, softly, gracefully.

See us, Meg?

"Isn't it crazy, Meg? Isn't it marvelous? After all this time.

You couldn't have turned up at a better moment, to help us celebrate."

In an ancient gesture, Meg's opened, tense hand sprang to her breast, as though to keep the stunned heart from leaping out. "But I don't, but it's incredible— Have I been all that much out of touch with everybody?"

She looked for a moment as if she were going to faint. She groped for the table edge, her ill, exhausted pallor under the tan, her short gleaming Apollo locks, looking like a parody of a healthy young woman in an apple-green linen suit on a summer afternoon. Sharing a very special reunion with an old and dear friend.

It was perfectly clear to Justin that somehow or other she had caught up with Bryn's side trip here and had come to find out, as fast as her schedule allowed her to, what it was all about. And from her reaction now, it was also clear that she had been expecting the worst: the walls finally crashing, the end of a world.

And Clare, with a resolution and speed and confidence which astonished him (a Clare whom he now thought he remembered, from way back when), had shown her in an unanswerable fashion that doom was not waiting for her in Parish Landing. Or, at least, not at this moment, not now.

It was a dazzling one-woman triple play. Bryn, no possible reinvolvement here. Clare herself, sweetly in the clear. Meg, reprieved and safe.

What an actress she is, Justin thought. But then she had had to learn to step out briskly carrying her colors on an earth that had shifted its balance under her feet. Acting would have been an art learned the hard way.

For verisimilitude, he leaned his cheek against her hair and crossed his own arms over her waist. She kissed his chin lightly and then said, "Get Meg a drink, will you darling? Oh, *Meg*—"

Meg had collapsed into the chair and had her hands to her face. Her thin shoulders were shaking. One ripping sob and then she dropped her hands, tears streaming. Relief had robbed her, Justin thought, of her crisp executive defenses.

Blurry gasped explanation, interrupted by a sad ridiculous little attack of hiccups. "I'm so sorry. God, I am a mess. We've been working day and night and I . . . Bryn hasn't been well, I don't mean he's ill but— When I heard he'd come straight here from Belgium I thought he'd gotten himself lost and was trying to find something, I was so frantically worried—"

She had almost said it; but not quite. People being given back hope and life can pour out their hidden centers before hearing themselves, before pulling back from the imprudent releases of joy to daily safeguards. She dried her eyes and blew her nose and got up.

"Promise you won't either of you ever tell Bryn about my attack of brain fever, stopping here."

Don't tell Meg, Justin. Don't tell Bryn, promise me. He had arrived in the land of don't-tell-anybody. And especially, while we're on the subject—leaving aside this married couple's troubles—don't anybody tell anybody if you know or guess who really killed Lelia Channon.

Meg's tone changed and warmed. "Let go of her, Justin, so I can hug her properly, we haven't hugged for years. Clare, I'm happy, so happy for you."

He went to get Meg's drink and thought it would be a convenient removal: Clare wouldn't want him listening to the first swift explanations, the necessary lies, about her newly minted love affair.

He lingered deliberately in the kitchen, bruising mint, measuring powdered sugar and crushing ice. He heard Clare's voice in the hall, coming toward him but floating the other way. ". . . for lunch, will you? It won't take any time to put it together."

She moved to Justin at the counter and murmured, "I'm terribly sorry. I couldn't think of anything else right then."

"Perfectly all right."

"And you wouldn't mind . . . continuing in the role until she goes?"

"Not at all."

"Don't go on sounding so polite and gentlemanly," Clare said, "or she won't believe that *we* are overcome by a storm of unruly passion."

"Shall we go on up to bed before you serve the salad?" His sharp and sudden anger took him entirely by surprise.

NINE

Over lunch—and it was salad, mainly crisp cold shrimp—Meg said, "It's going to storm. I hate storms. May I dither away the afternoon with you, Clare, and catch a dinnertime plane?"

"I'll leave you to your reminiscences." Justin finished his iced coffee, got up, and after a moment of thought bent and kissed the top of Clare's shining head. "Call you later, darling." He almost added in a warm immediate way, "Give my best to Bryn, Meg," and caught himself just in time. Don't tell anybody that you and Bryn picked up an old friendship, or found a new one, yesterday in Parish Landing.

He liked an all-out thunderstorm and felt one very close as he left the house in an unlikely plummy twilight at half past two in the afternoon. Cars were safe places to be, unless a wind-lashed tree decided to topple itself across your car roof.

The rain began its bucketing as he passed St. Mark's Church. To its right was the graveyard where Lelia was buried, in the Channon mausoleum. It was a properly Episcopalian English-looking graveyard, well tended, with brick walks and walls and tall trees, poplars and beeches. On a more clement day he might pay her a short visit. Preferably after a Sunday service, when by all and sundry the nephew of

the woman entombed could be viewed standing with bent
head.

Not only the nephew but a nose-poking writer fellow doing
a book about his family; even this ugly chapter in the Channon history.

There was a drenched orange cat curled demandingly at
Hannah's door, meowing for entrance. He had no idea
whether it was her cat, but it wouldn't hurt to give it shelter.
The door was unlocked, he found, while feeling for the key
Hannah had given him. She must be home.

The cat fled down the hall and into the kitchen. The house
echoed wth the storm and seemed to rock a little when a
thunderclap suggested itself as exploding inside the chimney.
Through the windows, in the near-darkness, he saw the lashing and heard the groaning of the grapevines.

There was no sign of Hannah. She might be one of those
people who hid under beds when a storm was overhead. He
went up to his own room. The door was open and his suitcase
was open, too, on the bed. When he had left this morning it
was on the closet shelf.

He put a hand into the inner side pocket of the bag. The
Clare note was there. Had it been taken out, read, and put
back?

As in some antique horror movie, while he scanned the
room for any other evidence of secret exploring, the closet
door opened silently, an inch, two inches.

"Justin?" Voice muffled in folds of clothing, and little-girl
high and scared. "I'm so glad you're back. Would you like to
come into the closet with me?"

Justin moved to the door and peered in. Hannah had returned to the back of the closet and was flattened against the
wall behind his raincoat. "I'm sorry but I—" Thunder covered
up part of what she was sorry about. ". . . but when the lightning doesn't show, and you cover your ears against the noise,
you hardly know anything bad is happening. And your closet

is bigger and deeper than mine and nowhere near the chimney."

How did you ask a relative why she had been rooting through your suitcase? You didn't, couldn't, directly. Matters could, on occasion, be misted over with manners. Try, though.

"I don't always leave bags open all over the place, Hannah. I'll finish putting away things in a minute or two—I was in a rush this morning."

The next thunderclap sounded a comfortable distance off. Shimmering wet sunshine tossed with leaf shadow fell into the room. Hannah emerged, her hair in her eyes.

"Oh, your bag—I got it out to see if there was any laundry I might do for you. In return for your company and your helpful financial arrangement."

"Thank you. I saw a laundry hamper in the bathroom, suppose I just toss things in that."

"Fine, dear. Thank *you* for the use of your closet. Did you get my ham and cabbage, and my nails?"

He had forgotten all about her shopping. "No, but I'll do that soon. I came back because there was something I wanted, in the bag."

He watched her face. It registered nothing but placid relief that the storm had taken itself off. "Well, I'll leave you to your privacy." She went out and closed the door behind her.

He got out Shoale's prescription and Edna's message about Mrs. Stone's cold and placed them on either side of the note. It looked to him as if the handwriting was Shoale's; but the hand loosened and erratic with drink. He had ruefully studied his own writing when, after a partying evening, he thought he had a marvelous idea for next morning's work at the typewriter. It looked, as Shoale's did, like a raffish first cousin to the controlled and sober hand.

He very much doubted that Clare would go to Shoale for treatment of any ailment she might have, so she wouldn't recognize the writing style. And when informed about who it was who had threatened her, what would she do? Probably nothing, Justin answered himself. Or certainly not a trip to the police station, pointing a finger at the town's key medical man.

He could read the police mind, listening to her accusations. Well, what do you expect the man to do on the anniversary of that death, write you a letter of congratulation? Even if she were received with unlikely concern and sympathy, there was nothing concrete to extract from the words; the punishment suggested for her might be read as of a moral and not a physical nature. The best she could hope for would be a polite chiding, "Now then, doctor, no more of these letters, all right? She takes them up wrong. All upset. Women, you know."

She might, though, want to face him herself. And if not, she would be at least warned and know the face of the enemy.

"Thank you for your good work, Justin. No, I will not take a midnight stroll up a deserted lane with Doctor Shoale at my side."

He could not without her permission take on Shoale. And, if he got it, "Exactly what business is it of yours, Channon?" But wait. He did have a special standing as of twelve-thirty today. It had not, however, been clearly defined in his presence. Were they, he and Clare, lovers? Were they thinking at all of marriage? It would be helpful to find out, and right away.

But not in Hannah's possibly listening hall. He walked to the Piggly Wiggly at the far end of Main Street, bought Hannah's dinner makings, went to the hardware store for her nails, and then folded himself into a public phone booth.

"Two things," he said to Clare. "I think Shoale wrote your note. I'll tell you why later. And—I suppose Meg's at hand?"

"Yes," warningly, "very much so."

"Then I'll thank you for a yes or no answer to the following questions. Are we just at the moment carefree lovers flaming away in each other's arms?"

"Yes."

"Did it start in New York, when you spent the night at my apartment?"

There was a little, spontaneous choke of laughter.
". . . yes, most people would suppose so."
"Are we going to be married when our smoke clears?"
"No."
"Then that's it," Justin said, "for the moment."

For his date with Edna, Justin prepared to put on another
face. Man from New York, used to available pretty women by
the dozens, stranded in a Maryland town and looking for a
good time. Well-dressed, free-spending man, too. You say
your husband's away? All right, let's have a short spin.

"I'll save some of the fresh ham for your breakfast, Justin,"
Hannah said as he left the house. "Cooked long enough, it's
not at all dangerous even in summer."

There was only one car in the parking lot at the medical
center, the license plate identifying it as Shoale's. A black
Mercedes, not old, not new. He had his hand on the doorknob
of the waiting room when through a slightly open window
close by he heard the voices.

Distantly, from the doctor's office, "Have you turned off the
air conditioning, Edna? You forgot yesterday."

"Yes, it's off. Night, doctor dearest."

Shoale's voice, now in the waiting room. "And where are
you going all tarted up like that?"

"Mrs. Hannah Channon is giving a wedding shower party
and Mr. Channon is going to drive me there."

An amused snort. "Have him drive you to Miss Tankard's
instead. You might find your evening more profitable."

It took little imagination to gather that Miss Tankard's was
the town brothel. Edna giggled. "Oh, you!" and, "Don't muss
me."

The window was heavily curtained. Justin backed up ten
steps and then advanced on the door and rang the bell. Edna
opened the door. The room behind her was empty. She wore a
bare, short dress of silvery green satin that highlit her breasts
and thighs. She was freshly and lavishly made up, a smoke of

lavender on her eyelids, gold tips on her lashes, jasmine perfume breathing from her.

"Aren't you nice, Mr. Channon," she said brightly, loudly.
"Can we stop at the drugstore for my present? They have a
gift department." Getting into the car, she explained this. "As
far as nosey people are concerned, I'm going to a shower." She
patted one green satin breast. "I usually keep something
pretty at the office to change into if anything's going on after
hours."

This gave Justin his cue. He didn't know how open, or how
secret, this engagement was meant to be, while Willett was in
Atlanta. "Where will we have our drink? You tell me."

"Well, let's see. I have my position to think of."

He thought her position was, on the whole, flat on her back,
naked and waiting.

"There's a little place up in the hills. It's new. Kind of a
family affair. Turn left on Everidge and just start climbing."

"Is it quiet? I'll want to talk to you. I haven't told you
about my book." He told her about it. Her first reaction was
feelable in the very air: shock.

Did her next question explain the shock? He wasn't sure.
"But you're not going to put down all that awful story, along
with the rest of the things about your family?"

"Why not? You must admit it's dramatic."

Sharply, "Is that the only reason you asked me out? To get
my version?"

"One of the other ten," Justin said. To assuage any sense of
guilt at using her, he called to mind her testimony at the
trial. ". . . and then she said—before Mrs. Channon hit her
with the cane— 'But I'm your niece. I suppose he'll get everything. Where does that leave me? It's not fair. I don't know
how I'll stop it but I'm sure going to try.'"

If Clare was to be believed, and Justin believed her wholly,
this was invented in a fire of spite. Unless it was a matter of
personal fear, or covering up for somebody else, she had noth-

ing to gain by this tactic except perhaps the foot sweetly rewarded as it kicked the ribs of the prone helpless body.

In subtle cross-examination, Clare's lawyer had made it
clear to the court that Edna Coats disliked Clare Herne.

"Admire her? Why should I admire her? Everything done
for her, not a finger to lift, and being able to take three
months off work just to wander around and paint pictures and
read to her aunt."

He felt a hand on his arm. "Turn left after this gas station.
By the way, you didn't tell me, are you married, too?"

"No."

"At your age . . . and the way you look?" She still had her
hand on his arm. "Here they'd say you must be queer. Are
you? You don't *feel* queer." A giggle. "I mean, if you know
what I mean."

He turned his head to give her the requested response, the
smiling meeting of the eyes. He was startled by the rake of
the look from under the lavender shadow and the gold-tipped
lashes. *What are you really up to?* asked the look.

He realized he had two women here beside him, the village
Circe, married or not, apparently out for a high old time; and
a mysteriously intent gatherer of information about him, and
his presence in Parish Landing.

Casually, she said, "I heard you'd been out to see her. The
Herne woman. But then, you're related, I guess?"

"Not actually by blood."

"Funny word, blood. In connection with her. Does she
know you're going to put her in your book?"

"She has nothing to fear about the way she'll appear in it,"
Justin said, and then thought he had been imprudent. But her
venom had stung the sentence out of him.

"Family loyalty's a great thing," she said. "Speaking of that,
here we are. My brother Ed—he's a twin—runs it with a friend
of his. I thought the least I could do was bring him along
some business."

It was called the Devil's Disco, a long log structure in a

heavy grove of pines. "Dance floor's closed," Edna said in a proprietary manner. "The action doesn't begin till nine. But there's a nice cozy bar." The bar was small, dim, and noisily crowded. People, most of whom seemed to know each other, were dumping down after-work drinks. "There's Ed. Let's go say hello to Ed."

Justin had a strange feeling of being a message successfully received, or a parcel delivered. "Here's Mr. Channon, Ed, Mr. Justin Channon." And it was as though she had added with perfect clarity, "The Mr. Channon I was telling you about."

Ed Coats was a thick, strong, and oddly supple man of Edna's height, same eyes, same waving red hair to his shoulders, but a large splodge of nose in his peeling pink sunburned face. Laughing, Edna said, "Poor Ed, he got ma's nose, see it? Don't join us, Ed, he wants to be private with me."

They squeezed into a place behind a little table, where the orange plastic banquette turned a corner. A large ugly mongrel, rough dark gray with yellow eyes in a black-masked face, came over to greet or threaten them, Justin wasn't at first sure which. "Ed's security force," Edna explained. A woman's voice across the room rose above the high hum. "And by Christ I told her I'll wring your neck for you if you don't leave me alone, what do you think I am, a dike like you?" Country music on the jukebox, "There's a bull snorting / and roosters cavorting / and chickens squawking no no / too recent, it's indecent / but you, you, *you* / are my an-i-mal." It was an atmosphere which, when encountered, suggested even to the healthy of mind that life was not so precious after all; that it was shabby and meaningless.

What, really, did all this, a world away from her, have to do with Clare? Probably nothing. Perhaps everything.

Edna wanted Seven Crown-and-7-Up and he thought he'd stay with safe scotch. But, on tasting it, not so safe; Ed, behind the bar, had paid his twin sister's new beau the compliment of a triple or quadruple shot in his glass.

Justin asked himself who was using whom? Who was the manipulator here, he or Edna?

Put things back in proper balance. "Before we get to you and me, there's a question or two. You're a shrewd girl, you know this town backwards and forwards. If by any chance it turned out it wasn't Clare Herne, who would be your second guess?"

She gave him a hard stare. "You've got to be kidding."

"No, I'm not. Anyway, give it a try."

She took a long thirsty swallow of her drink. "All right. If she didn't do it, my second guess would be the man in the moon."

TEN

A floating theory began to firm itself.

Either she was convinced of Clare's guilt, or she was protecting somebody with all her might and main.

Herself? Her husband?

Her twin brother? (Ed, I'm in an awful pickle, can you get me out of it?)

She might be thinking, Everything was so nice here up until now, Clare shouldering the blame and the burden. And now comes this man with his notebook (Justin had taken it purposefully out of his pocket) and his intrusive, disturbing presence.

Shoale might even have told her that he thought his patient was faking it, was perfectly well, and wanted some reason for personal contact with the office.

Well, I'll show Justin Channon that I have people around me, people to protect me, in case he comes up with some smart-ass new idea.

"I forgot it was free-drink night here," she said. "Buy one and get the second for nothing. Everybody comes running to the trough. Let's have our for-nothing drink and then we can go on to where we can hear ourselves talk. Will you get them while I go to the ladies'?"

Ed Coats' friend, the co-owner, was at the near end of the bar. An American type duplicating itself so often and so accurately as to be considered something of a national caricature. Short-sleeved T-shirt relentlessly defining incipient breasts of fat, swelling beer belly above a low-slung ample belt, cotton pants with the crotch wrinkles of cloth under severe strain, duck-billed cap above a small round-eyed face. And a look of being complacently pleased with himself and the way he was.

"Let's see, you're free this time." He lifted the scotch bottle over the glass and Justin said, "Two ounces, fine."

"Any friend of Edna's." He poured four inches of liquor into the tall glass and plopped in ice. "Seven-and-seven coming up." On his way back to the table, Justin passed a foil-wrapped pot on a corner stand, tied with yellow satin ribbon and bearing a card with the message "Damn (!!) good luck to Devil's Disco." He dumped most of his drink into the pot; it would be no great shame if it impeded the growth of the hideous yellow-green snake plant.

Edna came shimmering back through the drinkers, stopping here and there to chat. He was amused by her lady-of-the-manor bearing. Lifting her glass, she said with continuing self-congratulation, "You look like Robert Redford or something, in this crew. People want to know who you are. I told them, just a friend. Let's drink up and get out of here."

In the car, she said, "It's a nice evening and I have a nice home. Let's go there and relax."

At his very slight hesitation, she grinned. "Who're you afraid will misbehave, me or you?"

"Let's find out," said Justin.

The Willett house could have been predicted. No Maryland romanticism of age and pillars and wandering gardens deep in daylilies, but an upper-bracket suburban style, the eternal ranchhouse given extra length by the two-car garage facing the street (this always reminded Justin, architecturally speaking, of bare buttocks presented to one's face). Brick, no doubt expensive brick, mottled grayish-red. Sleek lawn without trees, the usual nursery-superintended shrubberies mounding high and low across the facade, a curving path of white pebbles from the street gate to the front door, spaced flowers along it, hot little red-brown marigolds.

"You may as well put the car in the garage, no point advertising us," Edna said. "If you don't mind going in through the kitchen." He now saw a third Edna—the house-proud woman who had left far behind the tumbledown Coats establishment with its chicken-scratched yard. And he thought that one reason she wanted to show him her house was to take the gritty taste of the Devil's Disco out of his mouth. That's not really me, that's not the way I live. Here is the way I live.

Wall-to-wall carpeting, of course, the sink-into kind, pale green throughout. The decorating scheme somehow pathetic: huge pieces of costly and anonymous furniture, formal pelmeted velvets and Brussels-embroidered batiste at the windows, a mirror-topped coffee table, large paintings in rococo gilt frames depicting a mountain scene in winter, an autumn scene on a river, and a spring scene with lambs and a shepherdess. There was a large gold-lace fan in the empty fireplace, and on the mantelpiece above it a vase of peach-colored gladiolas, rigidly spearing the air.

She waited, watching him, and he was generous with his compliments. She flushed happily and said, "I did it all myself, although I could have had an interior decorator. Sit down and I'll get things."

He chose a cautious perch on an arm of the ivory crushed-velvet sofa, and got out his notebook again. It was time for a little literary dust in Edna's eyes. She came back with a silver tray holding two bottles, glasses, and a bucket of ice. "Gin for me, scotch for you. Will you tend bar? I forgot the water."

When she settled herself with her drink at the other end of the sofa, she said, "Are you really a writer? I've never met a writer."

"Yes, seven books. Children's books."

"But then, is this for children, the one you're working on?"

"No—I don't think the Parish Landing chapter would be very suitable for them, do you?"

"Is it still that—that you want to talk to me about?" She lifted a restless hand to her hair. "It was all in the papers, you can look it up. They put down every word of everything I said, everything I knew about."

He saw that her twin's hospitality was registering. She was a little drunk and her gin and water weren't going to act as a sobering agent. Get on with it before she went to sleep.

"Yes, I read all that. What I want is your picture of the life in the house as it was *before* the crime—the contrast, you know. Everything so peaceful. The guests who came to lunch, or for dinner, or for weekends. Ordinary everyday things, like the plumber having to be called in, or Mrs. Channon ordering new clothes for herself . . . The picture as you saw it would make her death that much more dramatic. I'm calling the chapter 'Thunder on a Summer Day.'" He was glad he wasn't reeling this off to his publisher. But he thought it was as good a way as any to establish his bona fides and get her talking, get her rambling. Get her to drop something unimportant, all-important.

He saw the struggle on her face. The temptation to bathe in this flattering attention to her every syllable, fighting with—what? She might be giving him an answer to this when she said with sudden haughtiness, "I've had a great many more important things to think about since then. It's all like wiped out of my mind." The banker's wife disliking being taken back to her servant days?

Then her mood changed. "Don't be such a stranger over there. Come sit beside me. Who knows, you might just joggle my memory."

"Give me a little more time to concentrate," he said. She could take that as flattery, too, but it was meant literally.

He felt he was maddeningly close to something, something

solid and sound, emerging from lurking shadows and uncertain mists.

Had Edna had another man at the time? A man whom she told about the quarrel and who had had some reason of his own, ready and waiting, to get rid of Lelia? The quarrel would provide perfect timing and marvelous cover for a previously planned act.

Or had her man then been Willett? Find out. Willett had never been called to the stand. But when a death occurs, the butcher and baker and candlestick-maker are not called in. Nor the plumber, the laundryman, the hairdresser—all the unseen cast of characters involved in any individual's daily life. Nor one's banker, even if you had wanted to see him the next day, the day after you died.

Edna leaned forward to pour herself another gin. It wouldn't do to lose her to alcohol at this strategic moment. He got off the arm of the sofa and sat down beside her. No sudden plunging attack called for. She wouldn't expect that from the Justin Channons of the world. An arm lightly across her shoulders. She moved close against him.

Her eyes, looking into his, narrowed suddenly, showing just a glimmer of milk-blue, then abruptly widened.

"I think you like her, the way you talk about her. Like 'she has nothing to fear.'" Her voice was sullen. "You're her style, I guess, and she's yours. Well, I'll tell you something about her I never told anybody."

"That's my girl," Justin murmured encouragingly.

She had, she said, borrowed Mrs. Channon's pearls the day before the death, to wear to a party. She said she just thought they were store pearls. One of the boys she danced with worked at Harmer's jewelry store. He said the pearls had been in in April to be cleaned and restrung, and that they were insured for forty thousand dollars.

"Well, of course I was scared to death, I hadn't asked if I could borrow them. I brought them back but she was in her bedroom all morning and then went right back in after she threw that fit in the garden." She pushed damp red hair from her forehead. "But I thought she wouldn't keep her door locked all night, in case she had a spell and needed help or something. So I'd just slip in and leave them on the dresser— that's where I picked them up from. It was late, two or so, I wanted to be sure everybody was asleep."

She stopped, and, as if in desperate need of fuel, gulped her drink. "I let myself into the kitchen with my key and went up the back stairs. Near the top step, I thought I heard a noise. I waited and then went along to where the hall turns a corner. I put my head around and saw Clare going into Mrs. Channon's room. The door was halfway open and the night light must have been on inside. She was wearing yellow pajamas—I can see it now. I saw the pantyhose hanging from her hand. Then she went in and closed the door and I turned and ran. Of course I didn't know what she was going to do, in that room, but I thought she might come out quickly and catch me."

Groping, in the first shock, he asked, "And what did you finally do with the pearls, the next day?"

"Put them in her pocketbook, she left it on the hall desk. The police had the bedroom and her bathroom sealed up by then."

"And why didn't you tell all this to the police?"

"How could I? Looking like a thief and all. How did I know they'd believe I only borrowed the pearls for one night and didn't know what they were worth? They might even have thought I did it, killed her I mean, because she caught me with them."

"And why are you telling *me* this?"

Her voice was increasingly blurred but there was a curious stubborn determination in it. "I told you I guessed you like her. Clare. And one of your own family—you'd hardly turn around and accuse her and ruin her. And, if for some crazy reason you did, I'd say I never told you anything, you made it all up. After all there's no one to hear us."

"There's that boy who saw you with the pearls."

"I told him at the time, forget it, and he said sure he'd forget it." She let the upper half of her body fall forward, as though in sudden exhaustion. Her hair tumbled over her bare knees. The green satin dress had slid itself up.

Here we go again, Justin thought, feeling remarkably weary himself. Another step along the dark path with the signpost reading "Don't Tell Anybody."

The sound of the car in the driveway was not at all unwelcome to his ears. He had no intention of devoting himself to the task of adultery to further his researches. Authoritative and practical, he said, "Edna, up! Comb your hair, company arriving."

"Oh, God." She dashed for her handbag. There was a faint thud as the garage door lifted itself up in response to the car's electrical request. Justin went back to the sofa arm and waited. In under a minute, a man appeared in the living room doorway.

He was a very tall man of probably six feet four, ungainly and lumbering even while standing still. His head seemed too small for such a large body. He had a curious skin for a man, fine and delicately tinted as a baby's; large mournful brown eyes and side-parted brown hair worn in a dip over his forehead that suggested great grandfathers in sepia, in family albums. His heavy-fingered hands hung limply by his sides.

The expensive suit looked London-tailored. On one lapel was a plastic-covered card of the kind that identified people at conventions. Benjamin Otis Willett III, Parish Landing Bank and Trust Company. Not surprisingly, his arches had given up the ghost after years of supporting that height and weight of bone and flesh. His feet, in large polished black bluchers, were obviously flat.

"Ben dear!" cried Edna. She had whipped her face and hair into shape and her voice sounded almost all right.

He looked, very slowly and silently, from her to Justin to the tray with the bottles and ice bucket on it.

"I had one of my bilious attacks, Edna. I thought I would

be better off at home." Solemn, exact way of talking, each sentence a pronouncement. "I called several times on the road, when I was overcome by nausea and had to stop anyway."

"Oh, my poor sweet bear, bed for you." "Bear," obviously a pet name, an intimacy. While apt, an odd usage of it, in front of a stranger. "This is Mr. Channon, Mr. Justin Channon. He's here writing a book about his family." The two men shook hands. Willett's was cold and damp to the touch and felt as if it weighed five pounds. He inspected Justin with what seemed sad surprise.

"A book? Oh yes, Channonville, the original family seat. I am very sorry, Mr. Channon, that at this time we are in no condition for company. In fact I—please excuse me." He turned a faint bluish color and made a hasty stooping exit. In the near distance, a door slammed.

"It takes him that way, all of a sudden," Edna explained unnecessarily.

A nice point of etiquette presented itself. Did you wait and say goodbye, very pleasant to have met you, to a man just out of a spell of retching and vomiting in the bathroom, and probably still wiping his inflamed streaming eyes?

Or did you slip out discreetly—your silent vanishing a furtive explanation of the drinks tray, the bare green satin dress, and Edna's tightly controlled but still visible drunkenness?

She solved it for him. "He'll want to go straight to bed. I'll explain about the shower party, and you being kind enough to drive me home from it. I'll say you're already late for a dinner date. And, about what I told you before he . . ."

"I know. Don't tell anybody. Do you think I would?"

In the car, he thought about Edna and the pearls. He was now ninety-nine percent behind Clare, just one inevitable human percentage point off. The wild random pierce of *"but what if . . . ?"* was firmly and instantly dismissed.

Find a clean simple explanation for the tale.

From Edna's point of view, it provided the strongest possible reason for him to drop the whole thing and go away. A terrible hovering threat and new, further disaster for Clare, perhaps this time conclusive. *If* Edna decided to be a brave girl and face up to admitting she'd borrowed the necklace.

Would this tie his hands, forbid him to go about asking authorly questions? If intently listening ears heard about whom he was seeing, what he was asking, would revenge be dealt out, not to him but to Clare?

He couldn't, though, leave her with this unseen poisonous snake to be stepped on and bitten by, any time, any year.

A feeling he had had while listening to Edna became a near-conviction. He thought she was not that bright, articulate, inventive enough to have made all this up on the spot. He thought she had had this story ready for years, had rehearsed it over and over.

For when? For what? For some kind of naked emergency that touched her closely.

For now.

ELEVEN

On his way from Parish Landing to Channonville, Justin invented Richie Channon.

Richie Channon was one of the grandsons of Ives Channon, and had grown up let's say in Fairfield, Connecticut. He was now in his early twenties, and a bad lot. A motorcycle wanderer, a user and occasional peddler of drugs. He didn't care how he laid his hands on the money needed to lead his undisciplined life. When he left home for good, at seventeen, he took with him bearer bonds his father had been going to put in the safe deposit box, fifteen thousand worth. The family didn't pursue or prosecute him. Good riddance. He had been trouble from birth.

He surfaced occasionally, trying to screw money out of aunts or cousins, female cousins. He never approached the men of the family. In spite of his dangerous and untidy days and nights, he was still a handsome boy, and when he was clean there was something angelic about his fair hair and large shining eyes.

Among Lelia's letters ("Looking back, it seems odd that no one thought to go through her letters") was one from Richie dated a week before her death. He was desperate; he had to have nine hundred and fifty dollars, and he would hope to be given it in cash when he arrived at the farm next week. Across the top of the letter she had written firmly, in pencil, "Absolutely not. Note: have someone give him a meal in the kitchen, like any tramp, and send him packing." There was no return address on the envelope his letter had arrived in, and thus no way to head him off in advance.

Richie was becoming so real that Justin could well imagine the scene between the furious boy and contemptuous Lelia upon her flat refusal.

The practical brutality of the killing—her pantyhose seized from the chair where she had shed her other underclothes—fitted Richie perfectly.

And this, actually, was what a closely-watched Justin Channon would be in pursuit of here, along with other family researches: any word, any glimpse, any whisper of this cousin's presence in Parish Landing at the time. Naturally he had kept it to himself for the moment. You didn't want to accuse anyone, especially a member of your own family, until you had something concrete to go on.

This evening would be a good time to discover the letter.

But not right away. With Edna's tale still smoking-hot, he might not be able to stop himself giving it intact to Clare. No matter how calmly and dispassionately related to her, it would appear as an accusation, and a documented one at that. Don't, except in a final pinch, tell her ever about how, in her yellow pajamas, she had murdered her aunt.

Yellow pajamas. Why did he find it so hard to envision her in pajamas? She didn't look like a no-nonsense pajama girl. Either the comfortable habit of no clothes at all in bed—but then she wouldn't have gone naked to her aunt's door that morning. . . .

Meg to Clare: "Darling . . . get dressed . . . the police will probably be here in no time. I think your white nightgown is hardly . . ."

Why should there be such a great wash of relief over him,

at such a little thing? He had known all along that Edna's story was an invention, a rehearsed invention. This was merely proof—a tiny but vital flick of proof—that he was entirely correct.

It was eight o'clock. He thought he would find something to eat while he simmered down and became able to clamp on official silence in front of Clare.

He was driving along a road which he later discovered to be named Windermere when he saw the dog in the grassy ditch. And heard its pain. Struck by a car, left to its anguish . . . He drove on for a second or two and then turned the car around, got out, and went over to the ditch. A large and beautiful golden retriever lay in a crooked bleeding sprawl. He took off his jacket and with infinite care wrapped the dog in it, tying the muzzle with one sleeve. He lifted it first by what appeared to be its uninjured front legs and chest. Close your ears to the sounds the dog made. She'd weigh at least forty-five pounds.

A car coming fast around a near curve just missed his car, which hadn't in his haste been pulled completely off the road. "Damned fool!" roared a man's voice and then the car swept by. He had almost reached the door he had left open when a radar police patrol car, probably on the hunt for speeders, came along in the opposite direction. There was a scream of rubber as the car braked, crossed the solid yellow center line, and stopped nose-to-nose with the Volvo. A tall young black jumped out, and wasted no time with questions. "Yes, you'll want the vet. Here, let me help. Easy, girl, easy." Between them, they got the dog onto the passenger side of the front seat.

Her struggling had ceased. Justin wondered if she was already dead, or in some faint of pain. "Where is the vet?"

"A good way up the road. Follow me." And the police car preceded him, siren on and roof blinker blazing, at eighty-five miles an hour down the narrow twisting two-lane country road. They turned into a drive beside a little yellow house and the policeman rang the emergency bell at the side door, coming back to help Justin in with his silent burden. The veterinarian, a round ball of a man, opened another door at the rear of the waiting room and said, "Here, on the table." To Justin's infinite relief he firmly closed the door in their faces.

"Thanks very much," he said to the policeman. "You wouldn't know whose dog it is, or was?"

"Indeed I do. She's Bunker Bowen's Mary Lee, and he thinks the world of her. How was it you hit her, smart fast dog like that?"

"I didn't. I found her."

"Oh well. Different story." He surveyed Justin with a surprised friendliness. "Blood all over you, but that'll wash. You'll wait? I'll call Bowen before I take off."

He dialed, listened, and hung up. "This is his drinking time of day. I'll get the station to see if they can hunt him up. Good luck," and he was gone.

After fifteen minutes the surgery door opened. "Bad, but I think we can save her," said the round man, Dr. Lighter, and went into the details of steel pins to join shattered bones, sutures, transfusions, and a delicate operation which sounded so grisly that Justin did his best not to understand what the man was talking about.

"I'll be up at least half the night with her. I'd like a deposit, some kind of assurance that . . ." That a no doubt thumping bill would be paid in full. This was not the time to protest that it wasn't his dog. Just go ahead and bill Bunker Bowen. He made out a check for the requested sum, one hundred dollars. Dr. Lighter frowned a little when he saw it was on a New York bank. And then he carefully studied Justin's gory but English-made pongee shirt, his tie, the cut of his trousers, and his blood-spattered but well polished shoes. "I suppose it's all right," waving the check. "You can call me in the morning, any time after seven. Fine animal, worth the fight."

The stained coat was handed back and Justin headed for Hannah's to tidy himself up. She presented an odd picture, sitting on the porch stitching away at a dark mass of cloth on her lap. A lighted candle stood on the table, its flame bending and dancing. The grapevines groaned faintly in the day's-end breeze.

"You'll ruin your eyes, Hannah."

He had momentarily forgotten his appearance and she cried out, "What's that dark stuff all over you? It isn't *blood?*"

"A dog, hurt, but taken care of now." He didn't want to re-tell and relive the last forty-five minutes. "I'm about to make myself presentable."

The candlelight made her face look bloated and pale. "You gave me a scare . . . There are phone messages for you on the hall table. Clare particularly wanted you to call as soon as you got back."

All previous records were broken when Clare answered her telephone immediately. "You were going to tell me about Shoale, Justin."

Weighed in the scales of the recent hours, Shoale seemed to him just now extraneous and unimportant. "I got a pre-scription from him and I don't think there's much doubt he wrote your note. You can compare both at your leisure."

"No, I'll take your word for it."

Hearing the quiet anger in her voice, he asked, "What are you going to do?"

"There are times when you must look people right in the eye, and this is one of them."

"And when are you planning to do this?"

"Right away."

"Would you like company?"

"Thank you Justin, no."

The next best thing he could do would be to provide the company unofficially. But first give her her chance to look in Shoale's eye, alone.

"I'll just see you into bed," Edna said, turning back the spread and plumping his pillow. Willett, who usually was neat about his clothes, threw his jacket onto a chair and unloosened his tie. His throat still burned and his mouth tasted terrible.

"A glass of water, if you will, and I can't take aspirin even though my head is aching, not with this stomach."

"Yes, you can, I'll put a bit of soda in with the water."

"We'll talk about 'bear' later, I'm not up to it now."

"Rest's what you want, rest and sleep. I have to run out for a little while, but I won't be long."

"Run where?"

"I left my bag at Hannah's. I cashed my paycheck today and you never know." She looked flushed and excited, something bubbling up inside her. A rising tide of alcohol making itself felt? No, her voice had cleared.

He would have liked her to stay at home with him, but stopping Edna when she wanted to do something was not easy. Looking like an immense sulky baby, he said, "All right. Don't mind about *me*. I suppose I can make it to the bathroom if it starts up again."

"You'll be asleep before I'm out the drive."

But he wasn't. He lay sweating, sorely tempted to call up Hannah Channon on the bedside phone and ask her if there really had been a shower party at her house. That Channon fellow sitting calm as you please on the arm of *his* sofa . . . but this new man wasn't his main worry as far as Edna went. If you could call it an actual worry, a shadowy thing that came and went at the back of his mind and had been doing so for three months.

But no, he couldn't call the Channon woman. Checking up on his wife. Undignified. Considering his stand in the community. Considering anything at all.

He got groaningly out of bed and put his clothes back on. They were damp and rumpled but it was too much trouble to search out fresh ones. A little fire started under his ribs. He tried, in the bathroom, to throw up but only managed to punish his throat.

He relied completely on his car as a normal thing and was unaccustomed to the exercise of walking, especially when he felt like this. So much of him to drag along the darkening road.

He passed Shoale's white brick wall, went another eighty yards or so up the road, and cut lurchingly through a plantation of birches, their boles luminous in the twilight. The covering birches let him pick his way, out of sight of the house, around to the rear where the garage was, behind the loop of poplars.

He saw with a sudden blast of heartbeats his car, or the shiny bronze back of it, in the garage beside Shoale's Mercedes. He put out a hand to steady himself against the trunk. His trunk, with his license plate below it.

He turned and shambled slowly back the way he had come. He was, he told himself, in no condition to face up to people—face up to Shoale. In the center of the birch plantation, a wild dim thought came to him: suppose she had slipped out of the house to get him some special medicine, or to ask Shoale's advice on how to deal with this attack. Or even get him to come around on a house call.

And put her car, invisible from the passing prying eye, in his garage?

The only thing now was to get home, and put himself and his heavy ear-ringing sickness to bed. The male Willetts had a bad heart history; his father was dead at fifty-five, his grandfather at forty-nine. Don't think about Edna, or "bear." Go to bed.

Dr. Shoale's house was a copy of a French country house, slate-roofed white brick with graceful arched windows. It was set well back from the road at the end of a long, straight white-pebbled driveway. There were Lombardy poplars moving in the wind on either side of the driveway, and going around to circle the house in back. Their tops were green-gold

with the last sunlight, but the high hill beyond the house held
it in the purple dark of near night.

Following some instinct she couldn't quite understand (the
possibility of his calling the police to arrest her for trespass?)
Clare left her car on the grass verge outside the low white
brick wall and walked forthrightly up the drive. One room
upstairs was lighted. The lower floor was all in darkness. She
paused at the front door, between two large stone urns of cy-
press which had, to her, a funerary look. Then she rang the
bell. Not a light social pressure of the finger but a firm summoning one.

The light upstairs went out. The window directly above her
head was flung open. Shoale leaned out of it and looked down
at her, standing very straight in her white shirt and pants.
What she could see of him was naked.

"Go away," he said.

"No, I will not go away. I will continue ringing until you let
me in. And then when you do I won't keep you for more than
a few minutes, I imagine."

With cold fury, "Christ." The window went down. She
waited six minutes by her watch and was about to ring again
when the door was opened. In other circumstances she might
have been amused. Shoale's hair was tumbled, his feet were
bare, his blue shirt only half buttoned. A powerful waft of
perfume, female, floated at her from him.

She walked past him into the wide hall floored with highly
waxed slate, and turned. Not a man you would want to have
behind you, when you were alone with him. Or, well, not
quite alone, the interrupted amour upstairs—

"I assume you have not come to consult me professionally,
so shall we spend your few minutes in the living room?" It
was on the right. He turned on one lamp and went to a cabinet between two of the arched windows. He took out a crystal
decanter and, insultingly, a single glass and poured the tawny
liquid into it. Going to a mirror, he smoothed his hair with his
hand, and swallowed whatever was in his glass, neat.

"Is this a closed-door kind of thing? A confession, at last, perhaps?" He did close the door. The windows were curtained in striped silk, with matching blinds pulled to the floor sills. Privacy indeed, an unnerving helping of it.

"Not a confession, a question. Did you send me a note early in July? Promising me in a vague way some kind of punishment? Signed Justice?"

She saw herself in the mirror across the room where he had tidied his hair. He was out of the mirror's reflecting range and her aloneness in it, distant, white, braced, was somehow alarming.

"Can you think of any reason why I should have anything to do with you, on paper or otherwise?" He had recovered himself and, she thought, was preparing for some kind of cat-and-mouse enjoyment. Thoughtfully, he did up his two top shirt buttons.

"It's in your handwriting." Justin had said that it was; therefore it must be so. She was not a simple or, of late years, a trusting woman. But even after so short a time he seemed to her unshakably trustworthy. The source, the rock. Odd.

"And how would you know my handwriting?"

"That's beside the point. If it were you, I should think you'd say, 'Yes, I wrote it and what are you going to do about it?' That would be part of the pleasure for you. The wriggling on the pin. If you can't *see* the butterfly's throes, what's the fun of impaling it?"

From another room, a telephone began ringing. Without bothering to excuse himself, he left the room. He was gone for five minutes. Clare thought about departing. They were getting nowhere. But there was something she still had waiting on her tongue to say to him.

The hall door opened again. "I was wondering on my way back to this fascinating interview how you had the nerve to come here alone." An easy kind of threat for a man to make, committing him to nothing, but chilling the listener.

Alone?

I am not alone, she thought, not really, not any more.

"No nerve required. People know where I am."

He helped himself to another drink. "If by any chance I had written you some kind of punishing note—let's play your game for a few minutes—what do you think you could do about it?"

"Report you to the county medical association. For the moment, I'd bypass the police. But in your profession, ethics still get a capital E, at least as far as public relations go."

Shoale's face lengthened and hardened, and his heavy jaw swelled.

"Do you imagine they'd listen to *you* in your accusations? You must have very little idea of your name and fame, and not only in this town or county."

"Worth a try, though."

Open rage took over. "You Goddamned murdering bitch, this is just the beginning. You're going to be my hobby for the rest of my life."

Justin, with a swift calculation of times and distances, washed away blood, changed his clothes, and allowed himself crackers and cheese in Hannah's kitchen before going out to his car. "Be careful driving," said Hannah from her rocker. "This blue hour is very dangerous on the roads. Be sure to turn on your headlights. Poor Mr. Vanner forgot and . . ."

"Thank you, Hannah, I will." Hannah, he thought, had a doom on hand for every occasion. He seemed to hear her saying, "Poor Clare went all alone to see Dr. Shoale and . . ."

On his way to Shoale's house, he passed the Willetts' and had a mental vision of a patient Hannah would relish: the banker in the grip of dyspepsia, or overcome by bile.

A convenient chronic illness to offer, by the way, in the event that you wanted to cover the involuntary rebellion of the stomach when hit by a shock of terror, or guilt.

He rounded a bend feathered in willows and saw the great plodding clumsy figure walking slowly toward him at the side of the road. A phrase leaped to mind: the walking wounded. Willett when passed was looking straight ahead of him, not at the car or its driver. The glimpse was brief but searing, the contorted face, the gargoyle mask hung against the gloaming blue.

Willett walking not from his house, but back *to* his house.

"He'll want to go straight to bed."

Shoale's place was about a quarter of a mile past the willowed bend. He saw Clare's blue Toyota outside the wall (why should an ordinary empty car have such a lonely abandoned look?) and took the Volvo to the front door.

He might very possibly be denied entrance, so why go to the trouble to ask for it. It wasn't the lockup time of night yet. The knob turned obligingly in his hand. He went into the hall, where a small crystal chandelier shed a discreet sparkling light, stood listening a minute to absolute silence, and on instinct chose the dark room on the left, the dining room. He was no sooner established against the near wall beside a corner cabinet when there were footsteps in the hall and the sound of a door, not the front door, opening and closing.

"I was wondering on my way back to this fascinating interview how you had the nerve to come here alone."

Or so *you* think, Justin amended. He left the dining room and went over to the opposite door, and listened attentively.

". . . you Goddamned murdering bitch . . ."

He waited for the follow-up brutal sentence to finish itself, let another three or four seconds go by, and then opened the door.

In another day, under another set of circumstances, honor might demand that he stride over to Shoale and knock him sprawling on the carpet.

Instead, he put on an amiable and slightly embarrassed grin.

"The front door was open, so I just . . . Clare, I saw your car outside, am I too early?"

"No," Clare said, "you're right on time. We'd finished what we had to say to each other."

He went to her, kissed her in a husbandly way, and turned to Shoale, who stood rigidly by the fireplace, his glass in his hand.

"Wouldn't you like to be the first to congratulate me, doctor?" He tried his best to look besotted. "We've only just decided—oh, a matter of hours ago. We haven't hit the wire services or the television cameras yet." His arm was firmly around Clare.

Shoale put his drink on the mantelpiece.

"I hadn't been thinking of you in terms of matrimony—or whatever kind of pairing up you two are considering. I was back with your allergy. Have you recovered from that?"

"Your prescription worked wonders. Absolutely."

At the word "prescription" Shoale's eyes went to Clare and then cold and flashing back to Justin. Making, she thought, the instant connection. ("And how would you know my handwriting?")

Justin's perceptive nose sent him a sudden message. He had, without being aware of it at the time, recognized and identified the drift of perfume in the hall. No, he couldn't pay Shoale back with his bare knuckles; physical violence was not his way. But there were other methods.

He tilted back his head and sniffed, visibly and audibly.

Shoale's bare feet: he didn't look like a barefooted type. "Oh, you!" Edna's voice in the waiting room. "Don't muss me." And—conclusions were sometimes things to be leapt to, not backed away from—Willett's face, painful to look upon, as he walked along the road on a very possible return trip from reconnoitering this house.

"Persian jasmine," he announced fatuously. "The white kind. For a moment I thought it was from the garden, but of course the windows are closed, air conditioning . . . The reason it hit me was that I gave a bottle of it to my stepmother for her last birthday. I forget who makes it. But let's see, who was I with today who had it on? Not you, Clare—" with a gentle inquiring sniff at the side of her throat, "you're Joy, or is it Nuit de Noël?"

Shoale emitted a dry coughing sound.

"But enough blathering. We'll be off, shall we, Clare? I can well imagine what a work day Doctor Shoale puts in—his waiting room's like Grand Central Station. The least we can do is leave him to his relaxations."

TWELVE

"Our alliance is coming in handy in all kinds of ways," Justin said as they paused beside his car. "Shall we hug fondly in case he's watching us off the property?"

Her cheek was very cold against his. Some kind of Shoale chill, and no wonder.

"I think we both know what my shabby trick when Meg arrived was all about—but this time?" She lifted her blue gaze to his.

"I heard what he said to you, or some of it. 'Murdering bitch' and so on." His voice was as light as if he were discussing the weather. "I was providing a very old-fashioned kind of protection. Even though you will say indignantly that you can take care of yourself, thank you."

"No, I will not, I will say nothing indignantly. You are, you know, Justin, a perfect lamb."

Justin wasn't sure he fancied himself as a perfect lamb, in this deepening evening, with this woman.

"And who do you think was wearing the perfume, and waiting patiently for the doctor to come back to bed?"

There could be other wearers of white jasmine who might be involved with Shoale, but he didn't think so. However, turn it aside. "I was only telling him I knew there was someone there and in what capacity. And now suppose I take you somewhere crowded to dinner. The whole town might as well get the message while we're at it."

"I'd love to but there's a man coming to a late dinner who . . ."

Well, yes, why not? Of course. There would be a man, wherever Clare shed her throwaway golden light, here or in Paris. Strange he hadn't noticed until now that, on and off, she was shining again, with the light he thought had long ago been blown out.

Meg got home a little after eleven. She had telephoned Bryn from the airport in Washington, giving him her arrival time, her love, and nothing else. He usually waited up for her when she came home late from a working trip. He hadn't, this time. Their bedroom door was closed.

He had left the living room lights on for her. A big, mon-eyed room, lovely things everywhere she looked. The hang-ing-basket fuchsias in the immense tall windows looked as if they could use a bit of watering, but everything else was in House and Garden order. The apartment had, as a matter of fact, been given five pages in color in the May issue of that publication. *"How contemporary young marrieds created a glen of green peace high above the crash of the city."*

Tired as she was, what she called her body housekeeping must be attended to. A hot bath loaded with scented oil; her skin was inclined to dryness. Afterwards, in the dressing room, fifteen minutes of her ballet exercises. They had begun shoot-ing at six this morning and she hadn't had time to do them then. Four minutes with her teeth and gums: massage, roll-brushing, hot salt water rinse, dental floss. Eye cream, which insisted that it be patted in, not just stroked on.

Her heart began to pound when she took the blue drift of nightgown from the dressing room closet and slipped it over

her head. Her breathing quickened. She opened the door into
the big bedroom and turned on the lamp beside her bed.

Bryn in his bed had his back to her. He stirred, turned over,
leaned up on one elbow and yawned. "Welcome home."

She went over to kiss him. "I'm sorry I waked you, but as
long as I did I have a little budget of news."

"Good or bad?"

"Good, I'd say. I called Aunt Fan from Washington to see
how her arthritis is and she was bursting with it. The news, I
mean. Clare has paired up with Justin Channon. Do you remember him, from years ago? His own wife drowned or something."

"Oh."

Bryn put a shielding hand over his eyes. Perhaps the gesture of the sleeper startled from darkness into the glare and
discomfort of the light?

"They look so marvelous and *right* together—"

"How do you know that?"

"Fan said so."

"Oh."

She tossed the spread to the foot of the bed, wondering if
he would really welcome her home, with his body.

He took his hand away from his eyes. They looked very
dark and quite blank. Surely not shock?

"What exactly do you mean by pairing up?"

"Last I heard, there was only one way to do it." Her laugh
had a nervous edge. "Or do you mean, permanently? It
sounds very much like that to me. Clare's no child, and she's
always struck me as a rather constant person."

Wrong thing to say, somehow. She felt the hot color coming
up under her skin.

He threw back his sheet and picked up his pillow. "I'm off
to the dressing room. I have to be up at five—Boston—and you
need your sleep." Naked and graceful, he crossed the room
and quietly closed the door behind him.

Willett exchanged unfaceable reality for unconsciousness with the aid of two sleeping capsules.

He woke from a thunder of nightmares at a little before dawn to find Edna's place beside him unoccupied. He touched her pillow and felt a piece of paper. Turning on the lamp, he blurrily read her note. "Thought you'd be more comfy with the whole bed to toss around in, so sleeping in the den. Hope you're better. XXXX, Edna."

Was she afraid her husband's embraces wouldn't quite measure up to Dr. Shoale's?

No no, push that away, none of that was to be thought about yet, not at this terrible heart-sinking hour, the hour death was so fond of.

And if he did face her with it, what would she say? "You know my temper, Ben. Awful, if I say so myself. We wouldn't want to get that started up, now would we?"

In other words, Benjamin Otis Willett the Third, I will do whatever I want and there's nothing on earth you can do about it.

He got up and took two aspirins. He'd have to sleep some more, to be in shape for his day at the bank; a directors' meeting this afternoon, a proposal he must deliver on the introduction of Checksave accounts.

"Bear." That might be safe to think about while the aspirins went to work. Safer, anyway. It had been an early teasing endearment of hers, small Edna and towering clumsy Ben. It had since become useful as a signal, a warning, known in this context only to the two of them.

In front of dinner guests, "McCullough's on the phone for you, bear." This meant McCullough, president of the bank, was drunk and prepared to be abusive.

Right after an afternoon lovemaking session on the vinyl couch in the den, Edna on her way to the shower, spotting the woman marching up the walk to the front door. "Bear dear, here comes your *Aunt Charlotte.*" So for God's sake get some clothes on.

But why "bear" in front of Justin Channon? "He's here writing a book about his family."

Was he planning to wash dirty linen in print? Put Lelia Channon into his book? And Clare Herne? He let out a sound between a sigh and a grunt and fell back into a heavy sleep.

Carrying his second cup of morning coffee to the telephone in the hall, Justin called Dr. Lighter about the state or the fate of Mary Lee, the golden retriever.

"She's well on her way back to the land of the living," the vet said. "Or plain and simple, she'll be okay, but she'll want to stay and rest here—and changes of dressings and so on—for at least four days."

What astronomical sum would that cost? Before he could put this into words, Lighter said, "Her owner's been located. He's on his way here now. I'll give him your name, shall I? In your position I'd want my money back."

"Yes, all right." In his preoccupation with the morning's work he had laid out for himself Justin forgot to add Hannah's address. But that was easily remedied, he thought after he hung up; he knew the man's name, Bunker Bowen.

He was glad he had come on Mary Lee in her ditch.

His next call was to the Parish Landing Bank and Trust Company. The switchboard gave him Willett's secretary, whose voice was solemn with vicarious importance. "This morning? He has rather a heavy schedule, I'm afraid."

So Willett had made it to work, in spite of his bilious condition, in spite of the face he had shown to the passing headlights.

"What name did you say? . . . Oh, in that case, let me check." A moment later, "Mr. Willett will see you at eleven o'clock."

Justin occupied the time in between by wandering around inside and outside Hannah's house, taking pictures with his Konica. A plot for the book about the grapevine house was beginning to form in the back of his mind. In another section, the brain devoted itself to Clare. Was her dinner guest the stay-all-night kind of guest? Come to that, who was he? He felt a powerful curiosity. Hannah might have been able to satisfy it but she had left a note for him on the kitchen table: "Mrs. Dillard had a coronary. I'll be at her house all day. Fresh ham for your breakfast sliced, in the refrig. Too much butter frying it is not good for the stomach, esp in summer."

Justin gave the orange cat a slice of the ham and neatly hid the other three slices in the garbage can. Fortunately she had not saved him a plate of cabbage to go with his breakfast ham.

He walked to the bank, which was only five blocks away on Main Street. Gray-painted brick, white Ionic columns across a deep porch, a handsome and trustworthy-looking structure. He was directed to Willett's office by a teller near the door.

The man who rose from behind the desk struck Justin as a fresh, pink-and-white, shaved and showered ruin. Something about the hang of the cheeks, the downward droop at the corners of eyes and mouth. But more than that, far more, projected from inside.

"Good morning." The five-pound hand extended again. "Sit down, Mr. Channon." A pleasant office, and large; there must not be squads of vice-presidents as in New York banks, but just this one man.

"Your secretary told me your schedule is heavy so I'll be as brief as possible. I'm glad to see you've recovered from whatever it was."

Willett studied his easy-mannered well-tailored guest with the face he put on when a substantial loan was being requested from the bank.

"Yes, these things come and then, thank God, go. You'll take coffee?" He pressed a button and in a minute or so a pretty girl came in with a tray. Justin picked his up, black, and Willett tried to pour cream into his. His hand was shaking badly. He managed to get the cup to his mouth but a gout of creamy brown splashed down all over his fawn-and-white striped tie. "They do leave you like this, though, all nerves." He dabbed ineffectually at his tie with his handkerchief.

"Two things." Justin got out his trusty notebook. "At your leisure—some evening, not right now—I'd like your reminiscences about how Lelia handled her money. I'm told she pulled off some very smart deals in land, here and in Channonville. Robert was supposed to be the financial brains of the family but after he died she apparently ran rings around him, piling it up."

There was a short silence. Willett looked down at his cup as though he would like to have another try but didn't dare. "Anything I can think of which doesn't invade client privacy—"

"I'm her family," Justin reminded him gently. "I think I can judge what should be kept private and what can be told. People love to read about other people making money. You were in charge of her affairs for, what? seven years?"

"Eight," Willett said heavily.

"Good. I can see you'll be a gold mine, to coin a phrase."

This maneuver would place a possibly guilty Willett in a frightful dilemma; withholding information on the basis of so-called client privacy would make him look even guiltier.

"And the other thing. I've been going through my aunt's papers and letters and so on—for material for the book, you know. Letters are particularly useful. I found one from her great-nephew Richard Channon, Richie he's called. He wrote her a week before the murder asking for, or rather demanding, a large sum of money, saying he'd be there in a week to collect it. *She* wrote a note to herself across the top of the letter, 'Send him packing.' He's what is known as a bad lot, a tough kid, drugs, the works—he didn't by any chance try to cash a forged check at the bank? Or did you come across him in any way? Blond, blue-eyed?"

Willett looked dazed with this flood of information. "But the police—but why wouldn't they—at the time of the trial, why wasn't—how is it no one ever heard of this boy before?"

"Nobody troubled to go through her letters, obviously. And he might have had good reason to keep himself hidden, I believe he's spent time in jail, and pushed drugs as well as consumed them. And if he got mad at her flat-out refusal—"

There you are, Edna. Now you have a comforting answer to what's eating Justin Channon, why he's slithering around town asking questions, why he doesn't think Clare is the guilty one.

Willett made a confused attempt to take charge, in his own office, under his own title. "I'd have been told if there had been any matter of a forged check. And no, I've never seen this chap." He got up and went to the window, hands in his pockets, seemed to think there for a moment, and then turned. "By the way, I've heard, I don't recollect who told me, that you're to marry Clare Herne."

Justin thought he knew who had told Willett. Edna, a mussed Edna, Edna of the white jasmine perfume, listening outside a closed door in Shoale's house. Or, if husband and wife were not now on speaking terms, it might have been the major topic of the morning in Shoale's waiting room, Edna holding forth to her captive but probably fascinated audience; and carried thence to the bank.

"Naturally," Willett went on, "you'd want to find someone else who might have—"

Anyone but your bride-to-be, any murderer at all, he was implying.

"Naturally."

"I'm sorry I can't be of more help. There are a couple of run-down boarding houses at the south end of Main Street. You might like to inquire there, if you're determined to pursue this—slender thread."

"I am." Justin got briskly to his feet. "He might have given a false name but he has the kind of looks people'd remember. No point in going to the police yet, without something solid."

"Do you think it's, mmmmm, kind to Miss Herne to open all this up again?"

"I think it's not only kind but necessary for her happier future. Thank you very much for your time. My regards to Edna."

The other shoe fell at one-thirty. Or one of several pairs of shoes, the missing mate of which might also be expected to fall in due time.

Justin, who hadn't had a decent meal since Clare's shrimp salad—and that hardly qualified as a decent meal—had driven himself to a likely-looking restaurant on Rumsey Road, half a mile or so from the farm. After his lunch he proposed to pay a call on Clare. If she still had company, well, it would be nice to meet and assess her guest.

He was eating a tender club steak accompanied by broiled tomatoes and fresh asparagus when he heard himself paged by a waiter in the doorway. "Mr. Channon? Mr. Justin Channon! Is there a—" He left his steak reluctantly. "Call for you, sir." The telephone was in a cane cabinet in the resturant's entrance hall.

"Justin?" Bryn, his voice careful, cold, and hard.

To give himself time to think, to decide what to say to Bryn, Justin asked, "How may I ask did you track me down here?"

"My secretary's been pursuing you by telephone since ten o'clock. Hannah's, library, doctors, dentists, Clare's, of course —you weren't there and neither was she—the Inn, three or four bars, and then when it got to be around lunchtime she started on the restaurants. Then she called me in Boston." A very full report; maybe he, too, hesitated to come to the point.

"Go on," Justin said quietly.

"It's funny. You struck me as that rare bird, an honest man. Is it true? Why didn't you tell me? Why didn't *she* tell me?"

"You mean, Clare and I?"

"'Clare has paired up with Justin Channon,'" Bryn said, obviously quoting. "'They look so marvelous and *right* together.'" The coldness had gone and there was rage and betrayal—and bewilderment—in his voice.

Where do we go from here? *But it was only to protect you, Bryn, Clare's idea, not mine.*

Dump Clare, deny her, tell the truth, put this likable man out of his pain?

And then have the denial shot back to Meg by her husband, to seep into channels and over telephones and soon hit Parish Landing, and Willett, and Shoale?

There's nothing to that story at all, the two of them going to be married. What are they up to, anyway?

"Bryn, I'm sorry. There was nothing to tell you when I saw you. We'd met briefly some time back, in New York. Haven't you ever had immense split-second things happen to you? I saw her the day after you left—yesterday—and that was it."

"Then how come it's all over Hagerstown, this fast? Meg's Aunt Fan ready to throw the confetti?"

"A phone call doesn't take long," Justin pointed out uneasily.

"But how would she have time to see how marvelous and right you look?"

Damn you, Meg. Why the embroidery? Was it just for fun?

No, there would be no fun in any of it for Meg, it would have been a painful business for her, too. To have to tell him, between the lines of her announcement, So you see, Clare is out of the question for you, forever.

It was not possible to execute a shrug over the Bell System but he found the verbal equivalent. "Well, it's a small world. Especially here."

"Something's wrong." A deflated exhausted sound to him. "I have this strange awful feeling, I don't know, of doom catching up with someone. Maybe me."

Justin was silent. What was there to say to that?

"In any case, just to clear my muddled head, and close the book for good, I want to look you in the eye, Justin."

It must have been a common phrase of theirs.

Theirs. Were they still *they?*

"And when will you do that?"

Bryn answered, deliberately vague, "Oh, let's keep it open. As the clock ticks and the crow flies."

THIRTEEN

Driving to the farm and Clare, he felt a complicated aloneness. It came dangerously close to a brief sense of identity loss.

It was the result, no doubt, of being other people instead of himself, a group of other people. Baying hound to the ruin of the banker, trying to do what? Force him out into the open if he had been safely hiding all this time in the dark.

Squire to Edna, who might be using him instead of the other way round. Speaking of using—used by Clare in an easy and confident manner, as if she had some inborn right to him.

Analyzing for Shoale—who now probably ticketed him as effete—the personality of a perfume.

And with Bryn, coming on as lovestruck, inarticulate about it. "I saw her and that was it."

He had never before had occasion to realize the taken-for-granted pleasure of wearing your own emotional and intellectual clothing, at ease and at peace.

He was walking up the terrace steps when the screen door was opened and something was flung at him. A Persian scatter rug, landing in a small cloud of dust. The woman in the doorway, middle-aged, plump, aproned, said, "Oh, I'm sorry. I wanted to give it a good beating with my broom, the vacuum doesn't do all the work needed."

All right, as long as she didn't want to give him a good beating with her broom. "If you're Mr. Channon, she's up the brook," the woman went on.

Up the brook? Up the creek? What was this new flight?

"She said she left bathing things and a towel for you on the guestroom bed. I'm Mrs. Keating, I do out the house on Fridays."

He went upstairs and collected the yellow cotton bathing trunks (whose were they?) and the towel. He thought for a moment and then made a roll of them to carry. This might be some obscure signal and he didn't want to undress now and walk into something with most of him bare and vulnerable.

Oh, for God's sake, he chided himself in mild disgust. It's a hot day. Nobody wants to hang around a house that's being turned out. A swim was a perfectly sensible idea. But still . . .

The brook lay far to the right of the house, beyond the crabapple orchard. He began to walk up the high bank. He had forgotten about brooks—the clear amber weaving and twinkling, the delightful lazy music under elderberries and willows, the swirling about and embracing of tiny islands with wildflowers, blue and white, growing on them and trailing into the water.

The willows grew taller, not just graceful saplings now but old, high trees. The brook broadened into an oval glinting pool, high granite outcrop on one side, a steep bank of ferns on the other.

There was a rustle of water and Clare came swimming around an angle of the high rock. Coins of sun on her wet hair, one of them falling into a blue eye looking up at him where he stood on the outcrop.

"Justin darling." It didn't sound city-brassy, the overused endearment, not in this green bird-singing place. It sounded disarmingly real. "You've been doing everything for me and I thought it was time I did something for you. I brought some cold chicken and wine for later."

It wouldn't do to tell her he had had his lunch. "I can't swim," he said. "Is it deep?"

"Not over your head except for the center. I'm standing up. It's not slimy or froggy or anything. It's nice and clean."

Distorted brown legs and arms under the pale amber water, and what looked from above like a black tank suit and very little of that. He took a few steps back, perspective providing privacy, stripped off his clothes and pulled on the trunks. Circling around to the ferny bank, he went down it and stepped into three feet of water, then four. Very cold water.

She swam over to him, stood up, and took his hand. "Come on, it's better when you're up to your neck, you warm up quickly."

Justin gave her a long thoughtful look. If he wasn't getting her message, he would soon find that out. He disengaged his hand, put his arms around her, she wet and cold and warm, how could that be? He kissed her with searching force. And found himself astonishingly transported and happy.

"What did you have in mind, in the way of doing something for me?" he asked. "I'm not at my best in the water."

"I was hoping to shake you loose," Clare said. "So cool, so calm, so kind. Seeing abstract justice done and all that. I summoned up my nerve to attack you where you couldn't shout for help."

All her lights were on. She lifted her face. "More, please." And after the lingering and well-exchanged kiss, "I kept wondering how you'd feel. You feel delightful."

And then, as if in a not very determined attempt to stop something rushing toward them, she backed away a foot or so, water gurgling around her breasts in the sleek tank suit. A black fantailed grackle flew over them, low, its wing shadows brushing her face.

"You seem remarkably lighthearted under a lifelong curse on the part of a doctor of medicine."

"I am. You, I suppose. I haven't, by the way, pestered you about what you've been doing on my behalf. After all, you've been here only three days."

"And this is no place for our conference, do you think?" He gestured with a wide joyful sweep of his arm at the grassy bank above the ferns, under the willows. "Let me see, you provided me with a very large towel. Are you sure there aren't snakes?"

Clare laughed and caught his hand and kissed the back of it. "No snakes. Only butterflies. Butterflies don't bite."

They climbed through the ferns and Justin went around to the outcrop to get his towel. Clare had her suit peeled off and stood golden and straight and slender, waiting for him in drifting light and shadow.

Ten feet or so beyond her, a great thicket of elderberries moved. A man's face, square and ruddy, peered through the narrow dark green leaves. "Oh, dear God," he said in distress, "I'm sorry I interrupted your sun bath." Then he saw Justin, and the color of his face became even more pronounced in a mighty blush.

He pulled back out of sight. Justin handed Clare the towel and she wrapped herself in it. From behind the elderberries, the voice continued. "I'm Bunker Bowen. I've been searching all over town for you, to thank you and say I'll pay you. But I can't do that now, pay you, because I have to go to Sharpsburg about the pigs before I'd have the cash to hand."

Clare's mouth corners began to quiver, not with distress, he saw, but with held-in laughter.

"But I wanted you to know I was good for it, and tell you how grateful I am," said the disembodied voice. "They told me at the police station you might be at Miss Herne's, you weren't anywhere else that I could see. I stopped at the door and asked and was sent up the brook. Will I call on you later at your aunt's? I heard you were staying with her."

"Yes, do that," Justin said to the elderberries.

"And I have a message for Miss Herne. Mrs. Keating says

there's a woman Mrs. Wade phoned and is on her way to the house. Now I'll say goodbye to you till later."

"That would have been nice," Clare said. "Meg's Aunt Fan. Out for a stroll, looking for me. And *finding* me." She was rapidly pulling on her tank suit.

He gave her a light but tender kiss. "We'll have to take the will for the deed. At least, for the moment. And now you might lead us to your wine. So far nobody has even drunk a toast to us."

Willett's weekday habit was to drive home for his lunch. He saw no reason to hand over his good money for a meal when there was pleasant food to be had at his own table. Edna brought her sandwich to work, but usually fixed his plate before coming to bed. Something cold in summer, covered with wax paper in the refrigerator, little casseroles to be heated up in the oven in winter.

Today, he hesitated. He had slipped out of the house early, shortly after eight. It wouldn't do to begin the work day with a plunge into a sea of flames. Tonight, when he would be calm and tired, was the time to have it out with her. And she still, one chance in a hundred, might convince him she'd gone to Shoale for help for *him*.

Abruptly, he decided to go home after all. If he began now to hide, cower, how far would he be running backward from her? It was she who should be running in terror.

What will Ben think, what will he do to me? But he couldn't do anything to her.

The house was hot, even with the blinds pulled to the sills. They never turned on the air conditioning during the day except on weekends. He went first into the den and saw the mess the normally neat Edna had left. Flowered sheets half off the couch, pillow on the floor, underclothes on the floor, and her green sandals kicked off in the center of the rug. The expensive green satin dress in a crumple on one of the two chairs they watched television in.

In the kitchen, he opened the refrigerator door and took out the wax paper-covered plate. A sandwich, not a daintily arranged salad or a plate of cold cuts with his favorite tender white bottled asparagus tips. Ham, heavily coated with mayonnaise which slopped down over the edge of the crust. Jaggedly cut crosswise, no lettuce, not even a sweet pickle. Had she forgotten he never enjoyed ham right after one of his attacks?

It was as though she was saying, her voice echoing through the house, Oh, to hell with it. I don't care about your lunch. I don't care any more about keeping the house tidied. I have something else to interest me. To hell with you.

His face purpling, he picked up the plate and hurled the sandwich into the garbage can. Without bothering to look for anything else to eat, he left. He had to get out of this house, this uncaring defiant house. A house that like his wife seemed to be rejecting him.

He went to the Parish Landing Inn and was led with bowing respect by the headwaiter to a table set for four in a quiet corner. "We like to see that you have plenty of room, Mr. Willett." The headwaiter waved an approaching waiter away. "I will take Mr. Willett's order personally."

It was momentary balm, the accustomed royal treatment at the Inn, the deference to his position and title. It enabled him to eat his broiled half chicken—just right for a delicate stomach, why hadn't she thought to leave him cold chicken?—and asparagus tips.

In the middle of a bite of chicken leg, a sudden convulsion almost overtook him, coming from nowhere, a desire to burst into howling savage laughter.

Here he was wondering why she hadn't given him chicken instead of mayonnaise-slopped ham when the real question, the real fact, was that she had probably, in his own phrase, given herself to another man.

Words he hadn't thought he knew, terrible words, came

into his mind, about her. About his love, his Edna. But he couldn't do anything to her no matter what she did to him.

Hannah's house, in the late afternoon when Justin returned, was empty. She must still be with her coronary patient.

He had been introduced to Meg's Aunt Fan, a handsome horse-faced woman, whose nose was almost quivering with curiosity. "And is it true? About you two? Meg's thrilled."

Clare gave Justin a wary glance and then in acceptance of current circumstances said, "Yes, it's true. After we've changed may I give you some tea?" This invitation made her smile.

"Some bourbon is more like it," Aunt Fan said. "As you are well aware, young woman. Keeping up with romance is thirsty work. A long, hot drive, but I couldn't stay away. I hope you know what you're getting, Mr. Channon."

The last nine words hung on the silent air. Fan Wade flushed and added, "I've known this one since she was four years old and consider her *family*, one of my own."

("And did you see them?" Meg asked her aunt over the telephone in the evening.

"Yes. He even looks well stripped down to bathing trunks. Not unlike his father but we'll hope without the same roving tendencies. In my day, even if it was thirty years ago, we would have gone swimming up there mother-naked. Perhaps they're afraid of pollution, wearing their bathing clothes? But then they couldn't have turned up to greet me in the altogether."

"It's a small matter," Meg said, "but *actually* you knew about them three or four days ago."

Used to family connivances, Aunt Fan agreed.

"And in your words they look marvelous and right together."

"Well," said her aunt, "they do. Put on my darling Bryn to say hello."

"He's not here, he's in Boston helping marry two banks. I

don't know how long that will keep him there, and in this
heat.")

On the cool green-dimmed porch, Justin sat thinking
quietly, about Clare and himself, and her flinging open her
private door to him. Not recklessly or desperately but with
what looked like illumined happiness and welcome.

Leave that for later, for dessert. There were things to be
done. Think about Edna and Willett. Daring of her to leave
him and his possible peevish calls for help; and go down the
road and into Shoale's arms.

Had she some hold over him that let her do what she
wanted, however outrageous? Or was it just that Willett
couldn't do without her, no matter how she behaved?

Give Willett this evening for recuperation—if he could ever
recover from whatever had brought him crashing down—and
then move in heavily on him tomorrow evening, brandishing
the notebook.

Distant thunder rocked. It brought back a recollection of
Hannah cowering in his closet. ". . . but when the lightning
doesn't show and you cover your ears against the noise you
hardly know anything bad is happening."

A thought began to form itself, huge, dark, and strange.
Perhaps it had been lying there at the back of his head for a
time, dormant. A closet . . . He tried to grasp the thought and
take an unbelieving look at it. And then lost it as a car door
slammed and he saw Bunker Bowen, and saw him whole as it
were, climbing the porch steps.

It was too wild anyway, a fantasy, the thought or rather
shadow of a thought: a product no doubt of the heat and the
faraway thunder, and the rising powerful pressure of his own
emotions.

"May the good God bless you," intoned Bunker Bowen
from the top step. "Will I sit down for a moment with you?"

"You sit down and I'll get us a drink. If you—?" A polite but
unnecessary half-question. Bowen looked and sounded as if he
had been celebrating something.

He accepted the scotch enthusiastically. "It's my sister, bitch that she is and always was," he said, and then clarified this. "She had the care of the dog for the afternoon and left the gate open, and Mary Lee ran out—she can't stand the woman either—with the idea of getting on home to me. They say you didn't hit her, some other bastard did. I mean, some *bastard* did. Pardon my French."

He got out a fat shabby wallet and produced ten ten-dollar bills, counting them out on the table. "There. But you can't thank a man with money, especially his own money, for doing what you did." He leaned forward in a conspiratorial fashion, lowering his voice. "Can we be heard here? Is there anyone in the house?"

"No one," Justin said, expecting a rambling tale of how the Sharpsburg pigs had brought Bowen this windfall of cash.

"I'm told you're writing a book, and I suppose you wouldn't leave out the sad sudden death of Mrs. Channon. I'll tell you something about that nobody's ever been told before, just by way of gratitude. Doctor Lighter told me how you . . ." Something like tears glistened in Bowen's brown eyes.

"I always had it on my conscience, that pretty Herne girl, but then she got off, so it was all right. But as you'll see I couldn't very well open my mouth at the time, and it was just idle observations, nothing much to go on."

He had been on parole, after serving two years of a four-year prison sentence. A friend, he said, had stashed a consignment of stolen chickens in his barn (at this he winked at Justin) and he himself got all the blame. "Not that I mightn't have stolen them myself. I have no profession and live by my wits or rather my blisters. A ploughing job here, a house painted there, fences mended, gardening at the big places."

It was the second week of his parole. He'd met an old friend and they killed a jug and played some cards. Bowen, half-seas-over as he described it, went home and took a swipe at his wife and unfortunately knocked her down. "She promised she'd say nothing but I never quite trust her." Then, in search of more drink, or if not drink, rabbits, he took his gun from its hiding place and went off in his car. His misdemeanors began to pile up: he ran over one of Ma Coats' chickens night-wandering in the road. He pulled his car into the mouth of Zeller's Lane and got out with his gun. To his certain knowledge Zeller's Woods were full of rabbits.

It was then about two o'clock or a little before. "Zeller's is right next to the Channon farm, you know. I heard a car pull up, down a little from the farm gates. There was a kind of lashing noise as though he was putting the car behind that big old stand of lilacs, you may call it to mind. And I thought, my God, they're after me, and I hid behind a tree and listened. It was dark at that hour, no moon. I heard him walking along the road toward the gates. Sometimes your ears can see, if you know what I mean. Big fellow, flat-footed walk to him, clump, clump, clump. Well, I thought, none of my business, people arrange meetings on the sly at night, men and women do. I went off about my rabbits."

Then it had occurred to him that he couldn't very well use his gun, with his flashlight as guide. The big fellow might still be on the loose, wandering around, and might come to see what the disturbance was. He thought he had better go home and to bed.

He had stumbled over a long protruding root at the entrance to the lane and his gun went off. "To wake the dead," he said. He had heard a car coming and crawled into the underbrush by the road. The car slowed as it passed the lane and then proceeded onward. He had seen the driver by the dim castback of her headlights.

"Your aunt I suppose it would be. Mrs. Hannah Channon, maybe coming back from one of her sick or corpses."

"Coming from the farm? Or from that direction, I mean?" Justin kept his voice casually curious. His intensity of interest might scare Bowen off or dry him up.

"Yes. Now the whole point of this is—" Bowen did stop in his tracks and looked sorrowfully at his empty glass. Justin gave him another drink. "—is that I'm also told you have your eye on Miss Herne." He blushed again in recollection. "There are still people who think she's the villain. It might help her, in your book you know, to raise these questions. Two other people around, at that time, on that night. You can see I couldn't talk about it when it all came out, because of the drink, and the chicken, and my wife, and the gun, and me on parole. But even now I'd be afraid to let you use my name. You might call me an innocent bystander, or an unseen onlooker, or something of the sort."

"An authoritative source, as the newspapers say," Justin agreed. His heart was pounding hard and his breathing was momentarily difficult.

But he was curiously unsurprised. Had he known it in his marrow all along?

". . . *flat-footed walk to him, clump, clump, clump.*"

FOURTEEN

A few minutes after Bowen had left, promising he would bring a mended and recuperated Mary Lee to visit Justin, the telephone in the hall rang. An old, cracked female voice asked for Hannah and on being told she was out, said, "You'd be the nephew?" in an eager prying way. "Well, I'd best tell you then, it may have been you he was watching."

"Who?"

"Hannah knows I use my spyglass sometimes, my sight's not all that good." Defensive and preparing to be indignant if necessary. "I'm up on the hill, I mean my house is. I thought I saw a new kind of purple-colored bird on top of her chimney and in the natural way I looked around a little. There was a man standing outside on the grass at the, what would it be, east end of the porch."

"Doing what?"

"Looked as if he was turned into a statue. Or more like, listening to something, never moved a muscle. Stood back a foot or so from the vines."

"How long was he there and what did he look like?"

"I'd say fifteen minutes. He just left, out the back way. His car was in the alley behind Hannah's shed. The trees hid it and I only saw him driving away, dusty old black car but I got his license number." This invaluable crone with her spyglass supplied the number. "Nothing-looking sort of fellow, dirty old white T-shirt, big belly on him, a disgrace at that age." At her description, Justin all but heard the snarling music in the Devil's Disco and tasted the blast of straight scotch.

"You'll tell Hannah, will you? I thought he might be figuring out a way to get in later and steal something, but then he didn't move from that one spot."

He promised he'd tell Hannah and then stood considering.

Bowen said he hadn't told anybody about his rackety rabbiting night, and for some reason Justin believed him. Therefore nobody had any reason to follow Bowen here.

It must be he himself who was being watched, and listened to. How long had this been going on? He might at any time have noticed the fat bartender, Edna's twin's partner, but perhaps friends of the Disco took turns keeping him in view, say half a day on duty.

Whither he goes, I go.

Mostly a waste of their time but this past fifteen minutes hadn't been wasted. He went out to the porch and verified the fact that the massed vines covering both ends were visually impenetrable, green curtains without a chink.

Willett—and while it might be unfair to him, how many large flat-footed men did Lelia have in her social and business circles?—might always have wondered about that single, ringing shot in the night. Now, if he was correct in his assumption that watching him, trailing him, was on Edna's behalf on behalf of her husband, Willett would know. Know who the man with the gun was and what the man with the gun had observed with his ears, that dark night.

Bad news for Bunker Bowen. Not so bad news for him. The sharp edges of fact emerging from the mists of theory; the muscles of action on the part of the enemy, after four years of relaxed and contented silence.

And, forewarned is forearmed. It would be a good idea to forearm Bowen, whose favor to the rescuer of his dog might have ugly consequences, to put it mildly. He looked him up in the telephone directory and saw that he lived not far away, on Fetter Street. If he was going home at all, he would probably be home now.

He was. The passing on of the warning presented a difficulty: he could hardly name Willett out of hand, even though he was now pretty well convinced of Willett's guilt. He had an idea, however, that Bowen knew perfectly well whom he was describing but in some kind of delicacy didn't want to accuse a man he hadn't been able to see.

He was inclined to dismiss Hannah's presence on or near the scene as coincidence. Night care might be high on the list of her death-beetle duties. Or was it that he had begun to develop an amused fondness for Hannah?

In a few succinct sentences, he explained the position to Bowen. And was instantly understood.

"That'd be Johnny Kester, the fat fellow. They play dirty, that Disco crowd." Bowen paused, obviously to think. "Mary Lee will be back home early next week. She wouldn't let anyone touch me. I've been putting off a job in Dargan, digging a well and breaking my back while I'm at it. I'll just slip over there after dark, that way I'd see if I was being followed. And be home when the dog's ready for duty." After another pause, "You'd better watch out yourself. I didn't mean to infect you, like some kind of Typhoid Mary."

"I will," Justin said. "But they'd hardly—"

They'd hardly what?

He considered going to the police and then rejected the idea.

"I have information that Willett was secretly outside that house at two o'clock in the morning."

"And who told you that?" Bunker Bowen might—no, would —deny every word of it. "Poor fellow, you can't blame him, seeing he has a mind to marry the girl. Casting around for anyone else to pin it to."

But, pin it to Willett, of all people in this town? The majesty and authority of Money behind him. In the manner of his kind, he probably served on charitable committees, would be active in the upper echelons of Boy Scout matters, and could almost be heard in Justin's ear at the lectern at St. Mark's Episcopal Church, condescending to read the Lesson at Sunday services.

As for the Devil's Disco at his heels, he could well imagine the response to that. It didn't take a hardened cynic to know that police palms were often crossed by the Devil's Discos of the land. Open after hours, and God knows what going on, the fights, the drugs, the clink of illegally sold bottles in brown paper bags.

Even conceiving a completely clean police force, the reaction of Johnny Kester or one of his ilk when questioned: *"Following* the man. Last I heard this was a free country. While you're at it, sarge, give me a list of some other people I shouldn't be driving my car behind, on the roads of this town. Who in hell is Justin Channon anyway? He's new to me."

"And what were you doing standing around on Mrs. Hannah Channon's lawn?"

"I wanted to see what variety of grape that is, growing all over her house. And can't a man cool off? Is it trespassing you're after me about?"

In any case, he felt a sense of motion under the surface, a surging, an impending. It might be wiser in the center of this gathering storm to let the principal actors write their own lines and play their own scenes.

Willett, after stretching his work day by an hour, drove home at six-thirty like a man going to his execution. His rage had turned into a sick, heavy dread. The thing to be faced, and then a question mark of darkness beyond it.

What if he didn't say anything at all? Except, "And how are you this evening, dear?"

No. He couldn't allow himself to be eaten alive. Again.

He put the car into the garage and entered the house by the door to the kitchen opening from it. Dinner should by now be in preparation, but it wasn't. She was there, though. He felt her in the house.

"Ben?" Her voice from the living room. Frightened of him by now, probably. He had made a point of skipping his invariable lunchtime telephone call to her. Stewing in her own sins all day, in the very same offices with the man, with Shoale. Or maybe a swift snatched kiss when she came in with a patient's folder? It would help if the rage took over again.

She had put on a long peacock-blue at-home dress and he smelled her perfume, the jasmine, from the doorway. She had a drink in her hand. There was something wrong with her face. Well, why wouldn't there be?

"I know it all," he said thickly, not able to manage any subtle leading-up refinements. "I never thought I'd call you a whore." He felt tears starting and blinked them away. "Whore." His voice gathered volume, the tremendous voice of a very large man. *"Whore!"*

He went over to her and slapped the drink out of her hand with more force than he had intended. She screamed with pain.

Caution gave him a sharp kick in the shins.

"I had to get it off my chest. Promise you'll never do it again, and then it will never be mentioned again. I know you're younger than I am, and silly-headed sometimes, maybe it doesn't really mean that much . . . but he's *older* than I am."

She gave him a look at first stunned and then calculating. She got up and scooped ice cubes off the rug and put them back in the empty glass. "If someone's been snooping and gossiping— If you're talking about my dropping around at doctor's, on the way back from Hannah's, with some patient files he wanted, that I had in my bag, you've got worse things than that to worry about."

In a surge of relief which came all too easily and was greedily swallowed and digested, he heard the main body of her statement and all but lost the warning at the end of it. He put his arms around her and kissed her, then went and got another glass and made a drink for both of them.

"You'd better sit down," Edna said. She didn't sit, but began walking back and forth. "I had a call a few minutes ago, enough to scare the pants off me. Eddie didn't like the looks of Justin Channon—thought he might be up to something fishy here. He's been having him followed just to check."

Bewildered and off-center, Willett took a pleased gulp of his drink and looked up at her. In his preoccupation with Edna, he had drawn a temporary curtain on the politely menacing presence of Justin Channon in his office. Keep it drawn. He couldn't face anything else large and terrible, not right now. Channon's tale of that boy Richie Channon . . . Well, why not? And his wanting an interview about her land ventures, again, why not? Perfectly natural; he had been a rather important person in her life financially speaking. He'd given her some of the inside tips himself.

Tight-lipped, Edna went on. "Bunker Bowen went to see Justin this afternoon. It seems he was around that night, hiding, in Zeller's Woods. He heard things. The car being pulled behind the lilacs and the special way the man walked. Flat-footed, he said. Big man, he said."

It was through a thudding in his ears that Willett heard the adjectives describing him. He tried to speak but his voice caught in his throat.

"You've got to do something." She was pacing again. "Bowen's nobody, been in jail, a drunk on and off, a hired hand, who'd believe Bowen against you? But Justin Channon . . . Now he's really got something to write down in that notebook."

Always slow in reaction to any sudden turn of events, Willett could manage only a stammered, "But—but—*Edna*—"

Her voice seemed to be coming from a distance. "Of course I thanked him, offhanded you know, for the call, and said that even though we all know who did it I was glad my own pair of big flat feet happened to be in bed with me at the time. Then I said it sounded to me as if Bunker was maybe trying to sell him some made-up idea to put in his book. They were talking about money, a hundred dollars. Johnny's always a bit gone with beer—he said the whole thing didn't make much sense to him either but he thought he'd pass it along. I suppose to impress Eddie that he's really on the job and not hanging around in the nearest bar."

She drank from her glass until it was empty. "Just like Bunker, Johnny's nothing. And he's Eddie's man all the way. But Justin Channon isn't nothing. Jesus, Ben, pay attention, you look like somebody shot you in the stomach. Listen to me."

Ben listened.

"He didn't go running right off to the police station. Johnny waited next street over, then followed his Volvo when he came out of the house. He went to the Sound Stage and came out in a few minutes with a tape recorder, must have been rented because it wasn't in a box. Then he stopped at Connelly's Gym and came out with some weights. Then he went out to the farm."

Willett blinked several times and gave a great exhausted sigh.

"Sit up, Ben. Don't just slump like that. Ben, *listen* to me."

After he had shakily managed the second drink he never allowed himself, Willett thought that more than anything else in the world he needed a shower, to clear the rumbling in his head, and wash things away. There hadn't been time for a shower this morning, he was in such a rush to leave (all right, flee) the house.

Coming downstairs in a fresh suit, he found himself ravenously hungry. Still no smells from the kitchen. Edna called from the den, where she was watching the local television news, "Let's get out of here and go to dinner somewhere."

Crowds, people looking at him, maybe reading him. He couldn't face it. "I'm not well enough, Edna."

"You'd better pull yourself together," she advised coldly. "If not out, then I'll order in. If you think I can cook at a time like this—" She turned off the news and he heard her on the den telephone, calling McCartney's Oyster House, which had an expensive home catering service. "Two broiled lobster tails, don't forget a lot of butter and lemon. Two French fries, two tomato salads, two lemon meringue pies, two coffees."

Two, two . . . the pair of us. Husband and wife. Was she my accessory or was I hers?

In the shower, he had thought of a delaying action which would give him time to think. Instead of just plunging, or being shoved, into some kind of finality.

He told her about Richie Channon. "I wasn't aware of the boy's existence, but . . ."

She heard him out, her face hard and pale. He could almost see her mind racing.

"Okay—but then what were you doing out there at two o'clock in the morning? Or someone who sounds like you?"

Fumblingly, he said, "I'd—she'd told me she was frightened of him and someone else told me they saw him on his way out there, late, and I was just holding a—a sort of watching brief outside the house to be sure she was safe—"

"Why didn't you let the police do it? Money like that, a patrol car smack in front of the door wouldn't have been any problem."

He had the strangest feeling he was on the witness stand. "Benjamin Otis Willett, did you or did you not . . . ?" and she sitting up behind the high desk, in judgment.

"No," she said, the judge summing it up. "You weren't there at all. Like I said, Bunker doesn't count. And the way

we see it, one way or another no one else has ever heard
about it."

She lifted her long skirt and scowled at the great wet splash
near the hem. "I'm going to have a shower, too. God, what a
sweat this business is."

Willett, slumping again, waited for her on the sofa, bending
over, hands flopping over his spread-apart knees, head
hanging.

In his mental confusion, he was listening again to the horrible echo of the word, through the house. "*Whore!*"

But she had just been delivering patient files to Shoale. He
had kissed and forgiven her.

Then why had her car been in Shoale's garage?

He had forgiven her.

Perhaps it had been lying in wait for him these past four
years: a time of cringing acceptance and apology, to go on
from here to forever.

It's all right, Edna.

I didn't mean what I said, Edna.

Do as you please, Edna dear, don't mind me.

He gave his head a rejecting shake so violent it hurt his
neck muscles. Don't hang here on the sofa like a great broken
useless doll. He could still take matters into his own hands.
He spread the hands, at least once and a half the size of other
men's.

He could show her once and for all that he was operative,
and in control, the leader, not the follower. And was dangerous when aroused. Show her that he could take care of things.

Anything.

FIFTEEN

Justin left a note for Hannah on the kitchen table. "Going out to Clare's for a while." A while could be a few hours or days, depending. It occurred to him that Hannah hadn't been informed of his alliance, even though by now all the town seemed to have it by heart.

He debated packing his suitcase and then thought that would look to Clare, on his arrival, like a careless assumption of intimacy, of now having every right to move into her world, including a physical right. He had done her a favor, several favors, in the role of a man newly chosen by her; now, the suitcase would say, he was going to collect.

The time at the brook might have been inspired by impulse, or loneliness, or gratitude, and he didn't want gratitude from her.

He could always come back for his clothes. If.

The afternoon thunderstorm hadn't hit Channonville, rumbling its way instead toward Parish Landing. But beyond the immediate loom of the flat-footed man, Hannah hiding in the closet hovered close behind.

He stopped at the Sound Stage on Main Street to rent a tape recorder, and then did his errand at Connelly's Gym. It was after five-thirty, and the going-home traffic, for these quiet roads, could be called heavy in Channonville terms. He thought he saw, three or four cars back, what might be his spyglass crone's "dusty old black car" but in this or any other part of the country such vehicles abounded. When he turned in at the farm gate, he saw in the mirror a pickup truck, and a red car, and the black one, cutting to the left a good way behind, into Ferrier's Road.

But they would have no reason for doing anything to Clare. Or would they? "They play dirty, that Disco crowd."

Don't worry about her, she'll be okay, as soon as you get your ass out of here, mister.

The words sounded very real in his ears.

Mrs. Wade had departed and so had Mrs. Keating. Clare was sitting on the terrace steps with a watercolor pad on her knees, her china palette and blue-stained glass of water beside her. Justin walked up past her and looked down at her pad with artist-to-artist privilege. Green and blue, light and shadow, so fresh and swift it quivered on the paper. The focal point, the dim mouth of the tree tunnel, beckoning and mysterious.

"It's finished, don't touch it, sign it."

She smiled up at him. "I thought so, too." The slanting light turned her golden. He put a hand on the top of her head and stirred the loose shining silk under his palm. Her smile deepened a little.

"What may I ask are you doing with that machine?"

"That is between me and my Maker. Will you do something? Go to your room and settle down and read for a while, until I knock at your door? And if you hear odd noises pay no attention to them."

"Yes, all right." Not one question, just a faint lift of her right eyebrow. "Am I to have your company afterwards?"

"If you want it."

"I do. But as you're barring me from the kitchen, your dinner will have to be cold."

After she had taken herself off, he went up the stairs to the guestroom and plugging in the tape recorder placed it on the bed. He pushed the start button, left the room and scrupulously closed the door behind him. Even though he had wondered about that little oddment in Meg's testimony at the trial.

A closed door? On a hot Maryland night, when the through draft from the windows would be eliminated by the closing of the door across from them? In a house with two other women in it, her best friend and her best friend's aunt, known from childhood?

His own weight was 172 pounds. He figured Willett's as at the least 225. That meant a difference of roughly 53 pounds to be arranged for. The arrangement was in the trunk of the Volvo.

While not a man particularly addicted to any exercise except mile upon mile of walking, he was in good physical shape, endowed by birth without any effort on his part with a straight, strong, well-muscled body. He took from the trunk the two 25-pound steel weights, adjusted to the tearing pull at his shoulders, assumed as closely as possible Willett's slouched-forward posture, and went stealthily up the stairs. The weights held while walking upward imposed such a strain that he found himself barely listening to what sounds the stairs made.

The tape would listen.

He went into Lelia's bedroom, closed the door, went over to her bed, lay down on it, and made a not very sincere attempt to strangle himself with his hands. He uttered one cry, high-pitched, as close as he could make it to a woman's, and struggled. His head hit a rail of the brass headboard and with a savage twist of his body—surely no human being gives up his life without some sort of frantic final struggle—his heel thudded against another brass rail at the foot of the bed. After a few minutes, panting, he got up, picked up his weights, went out, closing the door silently, and made his way down the stairs, very slowly, very carefully. The heavy mahogany front door was seldom used in summer, except at night. He closed it behind him.

All right. Part One.

Returning to the guestroom, he pressed the tape recorder's stop button, put it on the closet floor, started it again, closed the closet and the bedroom doors, and repeated his performance with the weights. They were much heavier the second time. Up the stairs, Lelia's room, one desperate high throttled cry, the lashing body and feet and arms, out and down the stairs, front door closed. And the weights now safely back in the trunk of the car.

His arms were trembling with strain from his shoulders to his fingertips and sweat poured down his face, making a salty near-blinding blur in his eyes. He went to the lavatory off the kitchen to wash, the lavatory where Clare had rinsed out her bloodstained shirt. How odd he felt for a few minutes, without the weights—light as thistledown, barely fastened to earth.

The whole sequence, he thought, had taken perhaps twenty to twenty-five minutes. You don't hurry when you are trying to maintain a deadly silence in a sleeping house. There was no sign or sound of Clare. She must still be obediently reading in her bedroom. He reminded himself to ask her if her own door had been closed that night.

In the guestroom, he got the tape recorder out of the closet and listened to the playback.

There were five notable sounds on the first segment, over and above the dim grunt or squeak of an occasional stair tread. An almighty pistol-shot crack from one of the stairs near the top. The ringing thud as his head and foot hit the hollow brass rails. A thin but heart-twisting appalling cry. The pistol-shot again, going down. And the front door closing: even closed with the utmost care, in silence, some effect of air pressure or wood stress, or the stirring of a through draft from the rear of the house, set the pair of girandoles on the hall desk into action. The long dangling crystal prisms swinging against each other, in a sharp delicate singing and clashing.

The fault on the stair near the top might be recent, or decades old. The singing of the girandoles flicked his memory; he had heard them often, ten years ago.

An accomplished sleeper can take accustomed sounds at accustomed hours however intrusive. It is the unexpected noise which startles the sleeper awake.

He had read in the newspaper accounts of the trial that the lawyers for the defense had requested that Meg undergo a hearing test. Her hearing turned out to be that of a normal healthy adult of her age: keen.

Not for her an exhausting afternoon and evening, surely? The fifty-mile drive from Hagerstown, a cocktail and cold dinner on the terrace, and then a quiet time while both women read their books.

Why hadn't Meg said, on the stand, that she was a heavy sleeper? Nobody could have proved her wrong. But yes, it might have sounded forced, faked, a glaringly obvious attempt to help her friend.

He played the second, closet, segment of the tape. Or rather pushed the start button and watched the spool spin. There was for a short time no sound at all. Then the noise, muffled, the *crack* near the top of the stairs, but sounding like something heard from a considerable distance. And a ghost of an echo of the cry from Lelia's room, but he didn't think he would have known what it was if he hadn't been listening acutely for it. And finally a remote unreal tinkling such as a child might fancy hearing when Santa Claus's sleigh was flying high over the Christmas house.

He took the recorder down to the car and locked the spool of tape in the glove compartment. Going up the stairs again, he went along the hall, turned a corner, down two steps and across the landing and up two steps, and saw one closed bedroom door and one a little open. He heard music, Mozart. He called, "Clare?"

She came out of the room whose door was closed. "Honor system," she said. "I did leave you strictly alone. And I had my radio on, to give you even more privacy. In case of your odd noises." Her eyes were brilliant with curiosity. But he didn't want to tell her about it yet, if ever. It was something he had done mainly for himself. To test a theory, or a fantasy, a grotesque idea bred by an act of Hannah's and the sound of thunder on the far hills.

Listened to on tape, it seemed not quite as fantastic.

"Did you by any chance have your radio on, the night when Lelia—?"

"Yes. But not at all loud. It's an addiction of mine, I like to go to sleep to music."

"Was your door open?"

"No, closed. There are mice in the attic and they like to come visiting at night." She gestured toward the steps angling up to the right at the far end of the ell hallway.

He would have liked to ask if Meg had been informed about the mice, but if she asked why he wanted to know, her question would be impossible to answer. He guessed that she hadn't been told; people are not apt to advertise to their guests even innocent rodents. He settled for another idle and apparently frivolous question.

"Does Meg like to go to sleep to music, too?"

She understood him instantly. "Not that I ever knew of. Meg's quite disciplined, you know. When it's time to go to sleep she goes to sleep and that's that."

Being disciplined didn't necessarily mean being brave. Being disciplined might not force you to call out boldly, "Who's that? Who's there?"

They were standing in front of her open bedroom door. He looked beyond her, into it, and thought as he often had before that bedrooms were like diaries, journals, swift personal sketches of their inhabitants.

No attempt at a scheme of any kind, colors carelessly mixed as in an armload of flowers picked at random in the garden.

White walls washed with green from the maple leaves brushing the screens, low and well-filled bookcases under the windows, a comfortable chair, a book flopped open over its arm, a
wide bed with a white bamboo headboard. A strong sense of
presence, even though she was out here in the hall with him.

It would be a nice place to be in, with her, and very soon.

He put a hand on her shoulder. "Are we expecting anyone?"

She looked up and held his gaze in hers. "I'm expecting
you. I think."

"I think so, too. But first I want to take a short walk outside." This could not be left unexplained and she should be
put on her guard too. "I was being followed earlier in the
day. Edna's brother Ed's crowd. Probably just for general
snooping but not people you'd want sneaking around on your
grounds."

Very slowly and carefully, she said, "I see. Then were you
thinking about Ben Willett for your candidate?"

"Just as you've probably thought a thousand times."

She seemed to sway a little and he put out an arm to steady
her. He saw tears in her eyes.

"Sorry, just a . . . wave of something. Shall I come with
you on your patrol?"

"No, stay here." It was too difficult to think, standing this
close to her, and he had to think, and very hard. "If anyone
calls up, if company seems to be impending, tell them you're
going out for the evening and don't say where."

It was a little after six-thirty. A cool freshness was beginning to pool under the trees and rise from the grass. He
walked down the drive, through the tunnel of maples and the
orchards, and closed the gate. Not that this would keep out
any determined intruder—the fence was only six feet high—
but it did say to the casual Parish Landing eye, used to the
openness of the farm, "Not at home."

Looking down to the far right, he saw beyond where the
fence ended the great roadside mass of lilacs, probably the

pride of some long since vanished house. The lilacs that had hidden the car from anybody and everybody but Bunker Bowen.

This reminded him that there were any number of places on the farm, groves, outbuildings, sudden dips and rises of meadowland, which could be hiding a car right now.

But why?

In his usual fashion, he tried to put himself in the places and move into the minds of other people.

Johnny Kester would probably by now have passed on his overheard information; probably it would have reached Edna. She might dismiss it as thin ice, not for her and her husband but for nosey Justin Channon; nothing, really, for him to walk far on. Or, she might be panicked, sick and quaking, ready for any desperate enterprise. Wise to look on the dark and not the bright side of it.

If he had been spotted coming here, as he probably had been, he would be thought to be safely stashed for the moment with his love. His love, and his witness.

Had Edna told Willett yet? He might now be reeling under another mortal hammer blow, after stumbling onto his wife's adulterous evening. But short of the sweeping away of Justin Channon—which could hardly be done right under Clare's nose—what could he or they do about him, at least immediately?

And there was the near-sure denial on Bowen's part. Even if by distant chance he didn't deny it, the drunken evening, the knocking down of his wife, the stumble and fall which sent the gun off—what credibility would be attached to noises he thought he heard? And in such a blur that he might not even know what time it was? He would have to detail his evening and night in toto to the police to make it clear why he had not spoken out at the time.

He wasn't sure that he himself would have found Bowen's tale so dead on target if he hadn't been more than halfway convinced that Willett was his man. And that Edna was a

more than possible accessory, with her heaven-sent quarrel to
report to a man who had been summoned without warning for
a major financial accounting.

At best, they would conclude that no matter what odds and
ends of information he had picked up, there wasn't much if
anything he could do about them. Particularly with his powerful bias, committed as he was—first publicly and now privately
as well—to Clare Herne.

At worst, they would try to get rid of him one way or another. A beating-up by the Disco boys, get out of here or
else? Some kind of attack on him through her, perhaps her
house set on fire?

The civilized mind could not even circle around an ultimate
silencing. In this fragrant Maryland town, at this scented hour
or any hour from now—

But what was in the balance was the total wreckage of two
Willett lives.

The farm could in no way be thought of as a fortress. It was
accessible from all four points of the compass, and then there
was the natural and almost hidden roadway of the brook.

He walked a little way up the brook and heard nothing but
the evening silence falling, the birds muting their music, the
amber water gurgling to itself.

In some lights it would be a good idea to get out of here
and take Clare with him.

Now.

But that would leave the situation forever becalmed in
time, Clare forever question-marked, Shoale at her like a
cancer-carrying wasp. Even if you knew who was sending
anonymous letters, signed "Justice," there was no legal or
physical way to stop them.

Walking very fast, he headed back to the house. Clare must
have been watching from a window because she was waiting
for him at the door. Distress on her face.

"Bryn just called from the airport. He wants to see you. I

should have said you weren't here but I'm in no mood to disa-
vow you in any way at all."

"Oh, Christ," Justin said. And then he sighed. "What we do
not need right now is a chaperone. Especially that one."

From Boston, Bryn called Meg at shortly before two
o'clock. There was a long wait while her secretary searched
for her in the labyrinthine sprawl of the studio. She was
finally tracked down in a dressing room, triumphantly win-
ning a battle with a temperamental model.

"I won't be home tonight, Meg, just thought I'd let you
know."

"How's the bank deal coming?"

"Another conference next week."

"Then where—?"

"I think it's time I went and said goodbye to Parish
Landing."

SIXTEEN

Getting away from the studio at this hour wasn't easy, even
for a vice president, even on a Friday afternoon. Meg, nerves
jumping, deputed three meetings and a shooting session Saturday morning to her assistant Adela Howe, chosen by her because she was good but not too good.

Adela's eyes glistened as the reins were temporarily handed
to her. "Don't worry about a thing, Meg. See you Monday?"

Monday seemed a moon away. "I hope so. Family emergen-
cies don't seem to fit themselves to business schedules, do
they. Don't forget to tell them to pack a Thermos of non-fat
milk and scotch for Wicker, tomorrow morning. He gets nervous without it when he's shooting."

Cab to the apartment, a frantic few minutes packing, not
bothering to layer each garment in tissue paper, cab to Kennedy for the plane to Washington. Bryn would probably try
for the company jet but it might be otherwise occupied. In
that case he'd have to fly to Washington, too, unless by some
chance Boston offered a commuter plane service which made
a stop at Hagerstown. Unlikely but not impossible.

Explanations shouldn't be too difficult. "I didn't want you
to be alone, darling. I was worried about you. Your voice

sounded funny over the phone, raggedy edges." You couldn't really fault someone who, through love and concern, came bounding unasked onto the scene. Could you?

To stay away would have been impossible. There were dangerous things lying hidden under stones. The rest of her life, the survival of her marriage, might depend on the nature and course of Bryn's farewell to Parish Landing.

Just to see them together, to prove to himself that it was irrevocably true—was that what his journey was all about?

In the same way as, sometimes, you never deep-down accepted the fact that someone was really and truly dead, because you had never gazed upon him, or her, in the coffin.

She felt furtive, scuttling, as she made her way at a near-run along the endless passages at Dulles in Washington. As if by some wild freak of scheduling, his plane had just landed, too, and he would spot her, catch up with her, and furiously order her home.

This is my business, not yours.

Or turn up at her side at the car-rental office— But he didn't.

My business? Yes, of course, just to inspect the lovers and dispose of any possible inaccuracy in the report from Hagerstown by Aunt Fan. But looking back to her drink with Justin less than a week ago, it did seem odd that he had said nothing about it. Had been in fact quite detached about Clare, as if she was a casual acquaintance and not a woman he was thoroughly involved with. "She was down in my part of town and dropped in to see me."

And appearing not to know for sure whether Clare was on her way to Paris. Again, odd. But people are secretive about the strangest things, things other people would be shouting from the housetops. He looked, though, like an open man, with those clear and penetrating eyes. "Take off your glasses, Meg, I want to see if I remember you right." And then the sudden double blink of his eyes, an unmistakable flicker of visual shock. At the time, she had wondered why she couldn't

wait to get away from him and had been close to rude about
it.

It couldn't be some kind of plot between the two of them,
could it, the pairing up? Or among the three of them? And
against whom? Against her? Bryn's goodbye to Parish Landing really a goodbye to his wife?

You, my girl, are one step away from another attack of
brain fever, she told herself harshly.

She became aware that she was driving too fast, almost sev-
enty, and cut back to the commanded speed. Don't *you* drive
too fast, my darling Bryn. Don't let your reckless streak take
over.

It had appeared in the last year and a half, the recklessness,
the occasional weary I-don't-care face.

Time ought to take care of that, now with the door
slammed on his other, longer love. Meg had desperately
wanted the slam, listened for it year after year. For God's
sake, Clare, fasten yourself for good and all to someone, some
man. Instead of just dangling there on the far horizon, alone.

It was just before seven when she stopped in front of the
Parish Landing Inn. She had had her secretary call from New
York to reserve a room. At the desk, signing the register card,
she asked the elderly clerk if Mr. Hughes had arrived yet, Mr.
Bryn Hughes.

No, he hadn't, but he'd be told she was here if and when
he did come in.

"Don't tell him," Meg said. "It's a surprise." She went up to
her room, a double, because later on they might be sharing it.
Progress hadn't yet caught up with the Inn; the room was
large and pleasant and somehow personal with its bedspreads
and long curtains splashed with peonies, its grassy green rug
and cool white-painted furniture. There was a bowl of clove
pinks on the dresser, and the guest-greeting in a sherry glass
on a little pewter tray: iced fresh raspberry juice and brandy,
one single delicious swallow.

Clothes you have been distressed in, even leaving out traveling, acquire a nervous upset look of their own, she had often thought. She stripped and took a fast shower. No time for the long tub bath she really needed. Hurry.

Hurry where?

She didn't like the face the mirror showed her, the eyes too large, the mouth braced as if for a struggle. Clare when last seen had been looking so well, young and golden, fair and flushed with love. But she didn't have to compete with Clare anymore. Do your best, anyway.

Now what would be suitable to wear for an impromptu cel-ebration dinner with an old friend and her new man and per-haps one's own husband? Her bare-armed white, the one she'd met Justin in, fresh and easy and innocent. Loop the long rose-and-white striped silk scarf around the hips and let the ends float free. There. With her hair glossily brushed, and a fresh face supplied by Estee Lauder on top of her own tired skin, she looked all right.

She was not good at sitting and waiting, letting something happen and then catching up with it afterwards. Neither was Bryn. He would head straight for the farm if he didn't find Justin at wherever he was supposed to be staying.

And so must she.

Clare and Justin were demurely occupying the living room prepared for Bryn's arrival, she on the sofa, he in the chair at an angle to her, both being graceful and leisurely with their drinks.

"This is ridiculous," Clare had said as they arranged them-selves. "It feels like a stage set. If we're supposed to be wildly in love—"

"But we are," Justin reminded her, reaching out a hand for her wrist and then abruptly dropping it. "Too much," he ex-plained. "Even a little thing like a wrist."

"Just to get it straight, where we are now—first I used you shamelessly, and then you produced the same story, very nicely, to throw in Shoale's face. And then one way or another we began to settle *into* the thing, nature imitating fiction."

"You can scratch the word began," he said. "It's settled, don't you know that, Clare?"

"Yes. Let me try from this end and find if your hand is too much. And to Bryn—?"

"To Bryn as to everybody else. Plainly and simply, you and I."

Equaling his abruptness, she gave his hand back to him. It was an active ache not to be in each other's arms. There is a time when conversation, however murmured, however loaded, is not anything like enough. The flesh demanding to take over the dialogue.

"Maybe he's having trouble—" Justin began.

"Getting a cab," she finished, and a small gust of laughter caught them both, cut off as a car door slammed outside.

Clare got up and went into the hall, Justin close behind her. For a moment Bryn hesitated outside the screen door, a dark figure against dimming light. With one arm he was clasping a heavy paper carton. She opened the door and said, "Come in, Bryn."

He put the carton on the floor, took her in his arms and kissed her savagely, as though just the two of them were there. Clare jerked her head back and put a hand to her mouth. "For God's sake, Bryn."

"Well, it's safe now, isn't it. We're just two very old friends meeting." His eyes were brilliant, the dark blue looking almost black, and his face was set in a peculiar mask of merriment. Justin thought he had probably drunk quite a lot, on the way down, and was functioning in some sphere at one remove from reality. He was unwrinkled and immaculate in a tropical worsted suit, his pale blue shirt cuffed and collared in pristine white. Tall and fit and attractive to look at. The thick dun-blond hair smoothly brushed. And in some telegraphed way dangerous; perhaps only to himself.

"I brought champagne, if there really is something to drink it to. Is there, Clare?"

"Yes, there is." Slow and in a way unwilling, not wanting to scald him to his face. But final.

Now he looked at Justin, measuringly, icily. "Get some glasses, will you, mate." A contemptuous command.

"Clare, show me where they are."

"Clare, don't move. I have only a little more of you. If he's afraid to leave me alone with you in your own front hall what the hell do you think it's going to be like for him for the rest of all our lives?"

The rest of all our lives. It rang off the walls. Nothing, Bryn was saying, is changed between you and me, and never will be.

Justin went quietly to the kitchen and found tulip glasses, dusty, on a top shelf. He washed and dried them, and brought them with a large linen napkin into the living room. His face was calm and self-contained and showed no sign of the slowly rising anger underneath.

Not against Bryn. Bryn was too easy a victim, and could be torn into pieces by him, Justin, if and when he chose to do so. In a way he was glad that Bryn, in his love and loss and obvious despair, was not acting at all like a gentleman.

They were still standing. Bryn opened one of the four bottles of champagne, no fumbling or straining at the cork, a powerful pull, a popping that suggested close-by artillery rather than festivity. Without spilling a drop, he caught the first buoyant creaming in one of the tulip glasses. He handed it to Clare, filled the other two glasses on the coffee table, and said, "People stand around at wedding receptions as well as wakes and, so far, this is neither."

Clare sat down on the sofa and he took the place beside her. "I suppose I should get down to congratulating you, mate, if this isn't another game."

"Game?"

"Like the one you played with me the day before yesterday. Listening to my troubles, all but holding my head, father confessor and brother eternal. Remember I told you I felt as if you were my brother?"

"Yes, I remember."

"No wonder you wouldn't drive me out here, to Clare." A deep, bitter red suffused Bryn's face. "But not a whisper, not a word, to say, She's already spoken for, you poor bastard."

"Bryn." Clare put a hand on his arm. "It takes two, you know. Why not turn some of your fire on me?" But her voice was soft.

"How many times can you lose your faith in people? I suppose this is about the forty-ninth, for me. And then kindly driving me to Washington, to Dulles, because you said you wanted to see a girl there anyway—"

Pain for both of them constricted Justin's chest. All this because, long ago, somebody had really broken faith with everybody, including herself.

"—and seeing me to the departure gate just to be sure I wouldn't go to the men's room and take a dose of poison. And even then, when I was safely disposed of and not likely to come back here in a hurry—still not a word that you'd laid, excuse the expression, claim to her."

"We've been around this track before," Justin said. "I told you it was a sudden thing."

"You don't look like a sudden kind of man to me. But I could be wrong about you there, too." The knife edge left his voice and it became eerily light and sociable. "Well, what are the plans? A country wedding here? But you'd put her back into the press, locally at least, and the old story would be hauled out—"

"Shut up, Bryn," Justin said, sounding now a little dangerous himself.

"Or no ceremony, who needs that anymore? With a love like yours, solid as a rock, even though it happened in seven and one half minutes."

He turned to Clare and took her hand. "Swear on our

hands that this is true. That he's not playing some kind of Goddamned knight, protecting you from something or somebody. That would suit me better, about him—about the brother I found the other day."

Christ, he's only a breath or so away from tears, Justin thought. And how will any of this ever be put right.

Don't tell anybody. Was it time to heave that phrase into the fire?

Clare gave a shaky half-laugh. "That's a little along the lines of, Have you stopped beating your wife? Swear to you that Justin couldn't possibly be accused of any sort of kindness or bravery . . . He's being kind right now. I threw myself at him and he reached out and caught me before I fell."

And now, thought Justin, *she* is going to cry, too, and I can't comfort both of them at once.

The door of the car outside must have been closed very quietly. Meg's voice from the terrace startled them all.

"Clare? If you are in any kind of compromising position or condition, in there, I'm giving you time to disentangle yourself. I see Justin's car in residence."

She came in with all her flags flying, defiantly straight and swift, head up, curls springing and becomingly windswept. "Bryn." He had gotten up and stood staring at her numbly. "You beat me here but not by much. Kiss me hello, darling."

"Some other time, Meg."

She flushed and recovered. "I couldn't bear not to join in the celebration. Do I see some champagne left in that bottle?" To Justin and Clare, "Bryn said he was coming down and I wanted to surprise him and you two. Aunt Fan told me, Clare, and rather than telephone I wanted to be here, with you, to tell you how happy I am for you."

It was beautifully natural, the pleasure, the warmth, the old affection freshly rising. "As Justin hangs his hat in New York, we can be close again, neighbors I mean, how lovely."

He felt suddenly and enormously tired. His stairway voyages with the weights, perhaps. And that spiritual weight: it was not comfortable to have another man's fiftieth and possibly ultimate disillusionment millstoned around your neck.

The room was too full of emotions, the dark presence of might-have-beens hovering among them.

Bryn and Clare, a picture from way back when, handsomely beside each other on the sofa. Meg curled in lean, outward self-confidence on the loveseat, sipping her champagne.

". . . caught me before I fell." Was he, then, a choice made in some kind of desperation? A port in a storm? Did she still really want Bryn?

Edna. "And then I saw Clare go into Miss Channon's room. She was wearing yellow pajamas. I saw the pantyhose hanging from her hand."

Shoale: ". . . this is just the beginning. You're going to be my hobby for the rest of my life."

Were he and Clare about to, in this thick impeding mist, start on another gray might-have-been?

Bryn, looking suddenly ill, got up and headed rapidly for the door. "I suppose the lavatory is still off the kitchen." Parish Landing, Justin thought, was certainly not the place for an insecure stomach.

"Poor darling," Meg said. "The heat, and the excitement." It might have been anger at the parted pair on the sofa that made her add, "But back to you, Clare. What more fortuitous in the eyes of the great world than marrying a writer of lovely innocent children's books? I read one of the Don't Tells, Justin, or rather to be truthful had my assistant read it for me. And do you know, it *could* play like mad in the Saturday morning children's sewer."

Was it, finally, stung vanity that pushed him over the edge? He didn't think so. He went out to the Volvo, collected the tape recorder from the trunk, got out the spool of tape and dropped it into place. Rounding the house to the kitchen entrance, he passed the lavatory door, from behind which came distressing retching sounds. He carried the machine into the dining room across the hall and placed it, a handy electric outlet nearby, on the floor behind one of the tall folding doors, where it was well hidden from the casual view.

He wanted Bryn on the scene when the tape started playing. If he played it at all, if he didn't even now change his mind. But if there was nothing to his thesis—a politely modest word for his conviction of the truth of what had happened that night—no real harm would be done to anybody.

It could be explained, with a little mumbo-jumbo thrown in, as an amateur effort at a psychological test for Clare.

Who was and always had been, thanks to circumstances, a key figure, the heart and center of it all.

SEVENTEEN

"You're not eating your lobster, Ben." Edna said it a little timidly. He had turned strange on her.

He didn't answer but looked through her and beyond her as he buttered a soft poppy-seeded roll. A roll should go down easily.

It was perfectly clear to him that he had to kill a man, but he didn't know at the moment how to do it. Or when to do it. Tonight of course, sometime tonight.

They're not likely to give up the farm, he assured himself in practical bankerly fashion; and was pleased that he was able to think so quietly, so logically. She hadn't run away from it even when she was alone, but spent part of every year here. And Channon didn't look like a man who would run away from anything.

God knows what the place is worth now. Or, God and *he*. Five years ago Lelia had refused an offer of two hundred thousand dollars on the part of the architects Kitt and Kitt, who wanted to build a self-contained rich people's town which they assured Lelia would make Reston, in Virginia, look like a slum. Add today at least another hundred thousand to that. But to his certain knowledge Lelia had specified in her will that the property was not to be sold during Clare's lifetime; that if it was sold, the money was to go to the Ives Channon Pavilion of St. Hilda's Hospital in New York.

They would certainly spend time on the farm, on the scene here, for years and forever, Mr. and Mrs. Justin Channon.

He with his writer's powerful curiosity, coupled with his desire to clear his wife's name beyond question. *"I'd like your reminiscences about how Lelia handled her money. You were in charge of her affairs for, what? seven years. I can see you'll be a gold mine."*

As a family, the Willetts in Parish Landing were as old as the Channons in the next town over. Early sixteen hundreds, the Willetts went back to. Next year or so there would be Willett issue to carry on the name. Edna had said when they were married, "Give me five years to run around and enjoy myself, and then we can spring for a kid or two." People did not come down from the Northeast and undo Willetts. And, in the course of undoing, their chosen wives.

He looked thoughtfully at his watch. Twenty minutes to eight. Edna was pouring coffee into two cups and he said, "None for me, Edna, not at night, you know."

At his dead-level voice, she gave him another oddly anxious look. "But *tonight*—"

He got up from his chair and once on his feet felt for a second or so as if he was losing his balance. She saw the slight uncertainty of his body. "Expect me when you see me," he said. No goodbye kiss; it didn't seem quite decent to him right now.

She hesitated. It was one thing to think things and another to put them into words.

"Don't forget there'll be a car out at the back, behind the shed. In case you'd have any reason for not wanting to use your own car after you—to come home in. This one could take you out the back way."

"How wise is it to involve others?" Willett asked ponderously, the acute businessman, if a little awry, intent on office efficiency.

"He's just a poor slob who doesn't even know what year it is. Eddie can handle him. But he's good at driving, one of those tinkering car nuts."

Willett as always when leaving the house patted his breast pocket to see that he had a fresh handkerchief.

Then like a great crumbling pillar in motion, he went out to his car and went on his way. A man from a nightmare waked from his own long sleep, lumbering forward, heavy with danger, laden with death.

He wasn't exactly sure at first why he stopped in the parking lot behind the bank but it seemed a necessary thing to do, among other necessary things. Perhaps to get the feel of himself, authoritative, on top of things, totally in charge; that poor sot, McCullough, the President, only showed up one or two days a week. He sat down in his high-backed leather swivel chair, none of your cheapjack plastics, and studied the clean surface of his desk.

It would all be here intact, waiting for him, tomorrow. No . . . Monday.

The pen in its marble mount ready to sign papers dealing with matters of importance. Joan Gildersleeve softly on the telephone in the little open-doored cubicle outside his office, "Mr. Willett is tied up this morning, I'm afraid."

Tied up. Back in business. Healthy, functioning, showered, shaved, dressed in the dark blue suit he always wore on Mondays.

The dark final things gone. Everything attended to.

Yes, Edna. It's all taken care of.

His eye, moving about the cradling familiar room, found the rifle on its mounts above the mantelpiece. An antique rifle, his great-grandfather's. Willett was active in the Parish Landing Historical and Marching Society, which every May staged a reenaction of the ambush in 1780 of British troops in Zeller's Woods. For this event, the rifle was loaded with blanks but last year, after an unsuccessful attempt at a robbery of the bank, Willett had thought it might be a good idea to keep the rifle loaded with live ammunition. Perfectly safe, there on its mounts on the paneling. And you never knew in these savage lawless days when it might come in handy. He had been taught as a boy how to use it. All Willetts knew how to handle sporting guns.

He would prefer not to have to resort to the rifle. Noise, in the quiet summer night. Like the single, rippingly terrifying shot he'd heard nearby when he was walking up the road to the farm. A sound now at last pinned down, identified, by that drunken scoundrel Bowen. But it would be comforting to have the gun in the car with him. And other thoughts, other ways, might occur to him.

Even though, when you thought about it, the gun offered a sure solution.

He fingered the keys in his pocket, a complete set of keys for the farm. Edna had given them to him while they were waiting for their dinners to be delivered by McCartney's. "Lucky I kept these. I almost forgot I had them."

The perfect excuse for getting out of this room presented it-self.

Clare said, "I must find something for us all to eat. Except you, Bryn—but a cup of jellied consommé?"

Bryn, pale and red-eyed, had settled himself in Justin's chair, with a languid, "Your turn for the couch, mate." At Clare's suggestion, he said, "What a lovely long memory you have. I could always get consommé down for breakfast after parties. But there's no need to feed two uninvited guests. And our celebration is pretty well over, isn't it."

"Speak for yourself," Meg said briskly. "I'm dying of hun-ger and I've barely started celebrating."

Justin thought she didn't here intend cruelty but was play-ing her part as the happy wife, the happy friend, the sponta-neous and normal well-adjusted young woman.

He got up, went into the dining room, and pressed the start button on the tape recorder. Coming back, he said, "Sit still for another few minutes, Clare, it's time for your test," and sent her a cautionary message with his eyes.

"Well, then at least I'll refill my—" Meg stopped.

Little groaning creak, and then another murmur of old wood.

She put a hand to her throat. "Who's on the stairs?" She went to the living room door and looked up the stairway and came back, walked to her loveseat and carefully sat down.

Crack! The pistol-shot sound near the top.

"I didn't know you had a family ghost, Clare," Bryn observed mildly.

Clare opened her mouth, started to say something, and then closed it again, watching Justin's intently listening face. He had in hand about four seconds of silence now, while Lelia's bedroom door was being opened and the inaudible advance made across the rug, to the bed.

The more of a fool he appeared, the better. He said professorially, "This is a test of the weight of certain footsteps. I thought it might jog Clare's lovely long memory. Sounds she *may* have heard and mentally recorded even while she was asleep."

"Sounds from when?" Bryn had gotten to his feet. Justin put a finger to his lips.

The lash of head and feet against the hollow brass rails of the bed, an only half-heard struggle which seemed like an explosion in the living room.

Then the cry.

Justin, wondering if Clare was going to faint, moved close to her and took her hand and held it hard. But he could only spare her that one flick of a glance. It was Meg's face he wanted.

Her mouth had fallen open, grotesquely like the dropping of the jaw after death. But it had a purpose in being open. It widened and she screamed.

Bryn went over to her. "For Christ's sake turn that thing off, Justin, whatever it is."

"But I didn't hear anything like that," Meg shrieked. "Do you think I could sleep through that? Do you?"

Imperious, Justin ordered, "Be quiet! This is for Clare's sake. Now we'll hear the front door closing after him, Clare."

The unmistakable call of crystal, a fine musical clashing.

Bryn's face looked odd, the skin very tight over the bones. "What does the closing of the door have to do with the weight of certain footsteps?" The question was to Justin but his eyes were on Meg. Head bent, she was fumbling for something in her handbag and came up with her dark glasses. One of the earpieces caught in the leather strap and the bag tumbled to the floor, spilling its contents.

She scrabbled with uncertain fingers, picking up little pieces of herself. A slender gold perfume atomizer, her little red Hermes *agende,* a pillbox shaped and painted like a human eye. A photograph had been jolted out of her wallet: Bryn in white tennis clothes, sun-squinting, laughing.

This inner tremble—was it he, was it Clare, or was it both of them? Justin swallowed convulsively and said, "Be patient. Just a few minutes more."

The closet segment began.

"You may have to strain your ears here. But it's not a fault in the tape."

When the tape arrived at the faint faraway death cry, Meg writhed sideways as though to escape an invisible attacker and just saved herself with one hand from falling off the love-seat. From under the dark glasses, tears were pouring down her face.

In a talking-to-herself voice, wet, ripped, and breathless, she said, "I was frightened. Those awful footsteps, in the middle of the night, coming up the stairs."

Santa Claus's sleigh flew over, a frosty-night tinkle.

Her voice rose. "I didn't think. I couldn't think. I went and hid in the closet. I stayed there until I thought I heard the girandoles, or, yes, even a little while after that, in case he might be tramping around the hall making them shake." She looked, the taut efficient Meg, like a helpless boneless bundle.

"When I did come out there wasn't a sound. Everything was all right and *peaceful* is what I thought, then. I took two aspirins and toward dawn I fell asleep. I didn't wake up until I heard Clare, and knew something awful had happened from the way she sounded. And I went to help."

Justin noticed that Bryn had been slowly moving away from her and was now as far across the room from her as he could get. His hands were in his pockets. His face, devoid of expression, looked young and naked.

"But you see, don't you"—Meg clasped her hands against her breastbone—"that I couldn't tell anyone? Tell them I'd hid in the closet while Lelia was being killed? I didn't even know it was she crying out, I didn't know what it was, a cat, a bird— well, you heard, on the tape, would you know what it was? I thought if anything had happened, really happened, Clare would certainly have come running, but she didn't."

Silence.

A lightning mental view overtook Justin, the thundering implacable train set in motion by this little and not unnatural act of human cowardice—and the thoroughly unnatural silence that followed it. Unnatural and almost inhuman, even though Meg would have had to go through a brief hailstorm of embarrassment, criticism, contempt, and guilt.

Lelia's death might or might not have been prevented. A firm challenge from Meg could merely have resulted in a blow on the head for her, the death carried out anyway; or it might have sent Willett plunging down the stairs in panic, and out into the night.

It remained for the living to take up her burden. Clare, victim number one, on trial for her life. And afterwards, and still now, wherever she went, however she lived, on trial for murder.

Her union with Bryn, after the long love, seeming to be im-

possible then or ever. Bryn's next-best-thing marriage to Meg,
a sure summoning of future storm clouds. Still wanting Clare,
aching for her.

And he could have had her, free and clear, all the time.

He tried to dismiss the appalling question of whether Meg
had had a double reason for her silence. That, knowing Clare
as she did, knowing her to her bones, this accusation of
murder would make her back fastidiously away from Bryn,
marriage to Bryn.

Meg knocked her glasses half off trying to get a paper tissue
up behind them to wipe her eyes. "And then, there wasn't
anything I could do to stop it. I was stone stiff frightened out
of my wits. But if I had told them, you see that it would have
blasted my whole life?"

"So you contented yourself with blasting the lives of at
least two other people," Bryn said.

At the soft whip-edge to his voice, she stared at him
through the crooked glasses.

Justin thought she had hit bottom and was making some
kind of way back up. Anyone whose survival was so important
to her would have reserve upon reserve to draw on.

"Yes . . . for a little while, but it's all right now, isn't it? Everything is all *right* now."

"All right?" Bryn took his hands out of his pockets. "You
destroying bitch." He started across the room toward her and
Justin caught him by the arm.

It was a few seconds before the full impact of the words hit
her. She was saying, "Yes, I mean—Clare and Justin, and you
and I—" and then she stopped.

"What you and I? You've just wiped yourself out, or at least
begun the process." He tore his arm away from Justin's grasp
and took a step toward her. She reached for the strap of her
handbag, got up from the loveseat, stumbled and fell on one
knee, rose again and ran. Not to the front but to the back.
Three motionless people stood and listened to the screen door

in the kitchen falling closed and latching itself—that most innocent and evocative of summer sounds.

"Her car's in front, behind yours," Bryn said, pulling himself together like a tired general in a final and hopeless battle. "She's probably left her ignition key in it—crime around this house but not much in the way of theft. If it's there, the key, take it out, Justin. I'll go after her."

This time the screen door was hand-closed, not let swing shut. A deliberate controlled sound.

Clare said, "Hadn't we better go after them?" There were tears on her face now, and a blue-white underskin registering of shock and disbelief.

"I will. You stay here, in case she might circle and then come back, God knows what she might do to herself now, or you."

"I can't seem to walk, or move, or think at all."

He spotted the Waterford decanter of brandy where it always had been, on top of a tall red-lacquered Chinese cabinet. He splashed some into her champagne glass, worrying about her, hysteria possibly not far away, and said, "Get this down. Sit still. I don't really expect Armageddon but I'll go and see."

He went swiftly out into the overcast evening of pewter and violet, tree-massed with dim heavy green.

EIGHTEEN

Meg wasn't at first sure whether she was running from someone, or just away.

You destroying bitch.

Was she running from the bitch on the loveseat, leaving her behind forever, that thrown-away woman?

Could it be possible that she was running in terror from her own husband, from Bryn? That look on his face as he took one step toward her before she fled was a look she had never seen before.

"You've just wiped yourself out or at least begun the process." If he caught her, would he hurt her? Bryn hurt her?

She ran through the belt of maples in back, past the unused stables, across a rising meadow, heading to her right. She knew the property backwards and forwards but then so did Bryn. There was no time to spare to look back when you were in full flight, panting and sobbing, half-blinded with tears. Her thong sandals were light and thin, flat-soled, not the best running shoes but they were firmly buckled and couldn't be kicked off.

She thought about the brook with its high banks but then changed her mind. The brook could also be a trap, she could be looked down upon from above. There were intricately curving stretches of it but there were clear straight courses, too.

Away from the house, away, away, even though the long hills behind it to the west were steeper now. The thick trees were both a help and a hindrance, slowing her but partially hiding her except when they opened to embrace meadowy wildflowered places.

The overcast sky was getting darker. Too bad about her white dress, white advertises itself in the dusk. But when she had put it on she hadn't known it was a dress to flee in. She hadn't known Justin Channon was cheerfully rubbing his hands, preparing to ruin lives with a spool of tape.

If only there was a stopping place, a hiding place. Where her heart and lungs could rest. And for God's sake stop this moaning, this weeping, it used up breath and besides it could be heard if there was someone close behind her. If Bryn was somewhere near.

At the sight of a stand of sycamores up above, at the end of a grassy corridor flanked with willows, memory stirred. The tree house, built for Robert Channon when he was a small boy, and built so stoutly that Clare had inherited it during her early summers on the farm. It had been the children's favorite place because it was so high, on these hills, that you could not only see the farm spread maplike, but all the way to town, even a sparkling glimpse of the Canal. Picnics here, crunchy cheese-and-pepper sandwiches, iced tea, cookies; secrets exchanged, when Meg came to spend her two summer weeks.

The stairs were on the far side because the incline was shallower there. The tree house was an ample box six feet high, with long slits cut into it from which to view the great world and deliciously spot any approaching enemy, or parent, or friend.

Bryn knew the tree house, of course. One afternoon in June when she was thirteen his bare brown knee had touched and scalded her ankle when they were there hiding from Clare, she couldn't remember why. But at least she would be able to see him approaching, if he did come here to look for her. If it was anybody but Bryn, she would be reasonably secure. She could kick in the face anyone attempting to climb up the stairs to her.

There was a built-in bench along one wall. She sank onto it and leaned her head back against the wood, gasping for air. After a minute or so, she moved along the bench to the slit opening facing downhill toward the house.

No sound except the slight motion of the leaves, and a truck far away going down Ferrier Road. Not a sign of anyone in the deepening mauve-tinted gray. Unless he was behind a listening tree, or deep in a near grove.

He might have concluded her swiftest way out was through the maple tunnel and the orchards to the gate, and Rumsey Road, where she could thumb down a passing car. After all, a perfectly respectable looking young woman, not the kind of hitchhiker to leave standing. "My car broke down, can you take me to the nearest service station?"

She felt with fingers still almost nerveless for the condition of her face. Tear streaks, sticky. She took out her compact and set to work on the dim lavender reflection. No water to be had, so a few drops of perfume on a tissue to clean her cheeks. The perfume made her swollen eyes sting. A quick hair-brushing. Money to be counted. Seventy-six dollars, some change, and her trusty credit cards, three of them.

But what good would all this do her, here in the tree house? She could hardly go back and say, "I know where I'm not welcome, I'll just say goodbye and go out to my car and leave you."

If she went on up the hills she would reach, another three or four acres away, a road that she remembered as narrow and little traveled, Connister's. But that left her vulnerable, climbing the hills, the hurrying white ghost. And if she reached Connister's Road a cruising car with Bryn at the wheel—or Justin—might sight her and pin her against the gloom in a blaze of headlights.

If somehow or other she could transverse, manage, the three hundred-odd miles between here and New York, she would be in some sense all right. There was Eyeways, and her lovely job, and the big safe apartment, people around, friends, protection. And after his first storm of rage, Bryn might cool down and reconsider. Think her a coward and a sneak and all kinds of unpleasant things, but still his wife, still Meg.

Her eyes ached from scanning the gathering darkness, left, right, center, far horizon, immediate near mysteries of trees behind one of which there might be somebody. Far to the right, she caught a glimpse of a car, a dark car, no headlights, crawling slowly along one of the farm's several overgrown lanes. It turned off the lane and pulled against the side nearest her of a shed long fallen out of use; she had a vague memory of being told it had once held heavy equipment, ploughs and harrows.

The man at the wheel lit a cigarette and in the brief match flare she saw the one important thing: it wasn't Bryn. Or Justin.

Meg had always had a theory that there were two kinds of people in the world, those who coped and those who didn't. It was time to try to seize chance, and cope.

There was no point in puzzling about what the car was doing there. A tryst with a girl perhaps, a bit of snatched pastoral romance in the isolated shed. The thing was that it was there. She went slowly and carefully down the tree house steps. Covering trees promised to hide her on the slope that led down to the lane. Moving cautiously, pushing forward her bare toes so as to avoid trampling on dry twigs, she seemed to be listening not only with her ears but with every pore of her body.

The man at the wheel of the car was just discernible as a moon face peering curiously at her. Youngish, a hank of hair

falling into his eyes. A village lout of sorts, Meg summed up
instantly. So much the better.

She moved close to the car window. She smelled whiskey,
but that didn't matter.

"Will you drive me to the bus station in town, please? My
car broke down and I must get there in time."

Her voice was very little above a whisper. The lout said in a
clear ringing voice, "What? What's that you wanted?"

She leaned and put her face several inches from his. "Fifty
dollars," she whispered. She'd need her money and intended
to give him only ten dollars when he dropped her. No one
would think of buses. She was not a bus-taking kind of
woman. An hour's run to Hagerstown, and then the bus to
New York. Invisible gray people in badly lit stations, babies
crying, children shrilling, candy wrappers and ashes and cigar
butts on the floors, a dozing newsstand. And ladies' rooms to
hide in.

Teddy Varce's greed battled with his stupidity. "I'm supposed to *be* here for a while," he said. "That's what I was
told." His voice was not now raised but seemed to echo
through the evening.

"This will only take you a few minutes and then you can
come back. All right, seventy-five dollars."

"Oh hell, I suppose—"

She went around to the other side of the car. He let her
open the door for herself. There was sudden motion behind
her.

Bryn gave her shoulder a light push.

"Move over. I'll sit beside you."

Teddy Varce, switching on the ignition, said sullenly, "You
didn't say anything about two people. That'll be double."

Bryn paid no attention to him. The car backed and started
up the lane, toward Connister's.

"A hundred acres to cover," Bryn informed his wife, "is a
lot of territory. Lucky about the voices, and this car."

A matter of their own being talked about as if he wasn't the hell even there, Varce thought indignantly. Rich people. Couldn't care less about other people. He was tempted to stop the car and throw them both out. But, a hundred and fifty dollars. Maybe. And not more than twenty-five minutes to the bus station and back. Eddie wouldn't ever know he'd slipped out before parking the car behind the shed again.

Meg was totally unable to speak. Bryn beside her, the loved body, the alien voice.

"What I was really afraid of," Bryn said, "was that you would kill yourself, or try to. Although I should know you better, especially after the last hour. You could teach us all lessons in survival. So I had to find you to see that you made your statement while it was still fresh in your mind. And in mine. Justin's tapes are no good without you to verify them."

He leaned across her and said to their unwilling driver, "The police station, please."

Justin, who had been out for twenty minutes on a fruitless roam—ears on the alert for a woman screaming bloody murder —thought he might as well go back to the house and to Clare, who could now be in a crisis condition herself. Alone, very much alone, with Meg's voice still haunting the room.

"*How was Meg, on the stand?*" "*Just the way I'd be if the roles were reversed. Terribly distressed, voice shaking occasionally, color coming and going but mostly deadly pale.*" But she had been, finally, tough and brave in sticking to her betrayal, Meg had.

From the hills lifting beyond the house, he heard the sound of a car's engine. Not on the public roads. Somewhere on the farm. He went up a long slope from the apricot orchard, through an aisle of old twisted rose trees and junipers, thinking that from a higher elevation he might be able to spot the headlights.

He had neared the top of the slope when he waded into a little sea of nicotiana, dim white, a decoration of some forgotten garden. Their fragrance was just beginning to rise from these flowers of the night, a waft of sweet spice. The scent reminded him of something and to try to pull the memory to the surface he bent for a closer sniff.

The bullet wasped over his head at the same time as the sound of its firing crashed into his ears.

His body and not his brain dictated the instant earth-hugging fall. There were two more shots, and then silence, ringing silence. Could he have been wounded, even mortally wounded, and not felt it yet? Just as a bad burn, or a pierce of glass into the bare sole of the foot, take a split second or so to declare injury and pain.

He couldn't get up and run and silhouette himself against the heavy purpling sky again, as he must have done when he reached the nicotianas. Would there be more shots, aimed lower with deadly accuracy? The gun had been fired from behind, somewhere down beyond the start of the slope, he thought.

What had the man with the gun seen? A bending and then what he must conclude was a fall, because the body of his intended victim had abruptly been erased from the near horizon.

With luck—the other man's luck, that is—a dead or dying man might be presumed to be lying there, blood-strangled, soundless. A man merely wounded would be shouting with pain.

Wouldn't you want to see if you were right, and that you had killed your man? You wouldn't be taking any risk in this inspection, not with a rifle in your hand.

As he couldn't in any case get up and run, he decided in a swift desperate flicker his own strategy. He writhed his way, still flattened against the earth, to a half-guarded position behind a juniper whose thick lower growth draped into the grass. His arm swung wide, palm fingering the grass, hand praying for a fallen piece of bough, a protruding bit of rock, anything usable. With the blood drumming in his ears, he wondered if he would even hear the approaching feet.

If they approached. If the man hadn't turned and ran. What man? He thought he knew but it would be helpful in an ultimate sense to be sure. Helpful, though, only insofar as he was able afterwards to say, "It was Willett who shot at me." The alternative phrase, "It was Willett who shot me" could unfortunately never be uttered.

His fingers encountered something odd and unexpected and then sent him an identifying message. An old rusted spinner sprinkler, upside down in the grass, about five by five inches and weighing about a pound. Grippable, aimable. Better, a little better, than nothing.

Through chinks in the heavy dark lace of the juniper, there was enough light to see the towering clumsy man coming very slowly up between the rose trees. His rifle in the great hand hanging by his side.

The closer the better. If your heart didn't give up the job of beating while you were waiting.

Now. He rose inch by inch until he was kneeling. He leaned out sideways, toward the path, and hurled the sprinkler up into the face eight feet away. The impact, or the pain, or both, sent Willett staggering backward. He made a noise like a goaded bull. He fell sideways and tried to break the fall with one hand, his gun hand. The rifle was no longer in it.

Justin rose, took three steps, bent and picked up the rifle. Blood was pouring down one side of Willett's face. "Jesus Christ," said Willett with tears of pain starting, "you could have put my eye out." His voice was shaking, his face began to shake, and his whole body followed suit, one enormous head-to-foot tremble.

"And you could have blown my brains out," Justin said, and was surprised how hard it was to manage each word in turn. As though he had just run the ten-minute mile and, lunged out, was ready to collapse to the ground.

He saw the sprinkler near Willett's feet, picked it up, and threw it as far away as a suddenly powerless arm would allow.

"Rusty," croaked Willett. "Infection—"

"Come along to the house and we can get a doctor for you.
I suppose the police have one they use. Move. I'll be right
behind you."

Willett began a stooped shambling walk. "Be careful with
that gun. The safety catch isn't on."

"Let's just hope it doesn't go off."

"You've got this all wrong. You startled me so that I didn't
think to—"

"Don't stop, keep walking."

"All right. But that cousin or nephew or whatever he is, of
yours, that Richie Channon—someone told me he was heading
out here looking for trouble." Abject, shattered voice. "I keep
my rifle in my car, in the trunk, with the rest of my hunting
gear. He stopped his motorcycle behind the—behind a bunch
of lilacs down the road. I was following him, here on the
grounds, just to make sure that—and, getting close to the
house, I fired a warning shot over what I thought was his
head to—"

"Very helpful of you." More than halfway around the bend
as Willett was sounding, Justin managed in self-defense to
produce some effect of soothing approval and belief. He
didn't want to have to kill the man, even if he knew how. And
he might not be able to handle 225 pounds of around-the-
bend, suicidally erupting. "We'll warn Clare to lock up the
house good and tight."

"Justin!" screamed a voice to their near-right. "Justin, *Justin*." Clare came running in a rip of sobs. "I thought he'd shot
Meg, killed her, and I've been out of my mind trying to—" She
stopped short a few feet away from the two men.

"No, just a false alarm." Get her away from here before
Willett took it into his head to seize her as bodily protection
for himself. "Run on ahead, there's a good girl, and call your
doctor. Mr. Willett's gotten a head injury and needs attention
right away. He was trying to help out here and that's what he
got for his trouble."

She did run, and was on the telephone when Justin and Willett entered the living room. Willett said in a faraway voice, "I think I . . ." He sank into a chair, let his head fall forward into his hands, and burst into tears.

Still carrying the gun, Justin backed into the hall, very quietly, although he thought that Willett, tears and blood streaming through his fingers, was no longer even aware of his existence.

Clare had just hung up, and turned to him still clothed in terror.

"And I thought it might even be you, hurt, wounded—" She looked past him to the sagging, weeping man. Barely able to speak, vague, she said, "I'll get bandaging stuff in the meantime . . . shall I?"

"Yes." In case Willett, through his woe, was listening still. He took her hand and led her into the kitchen and pushed into place the heavy bolt on the inside of its door. He went to the wall phone and asked the operator for the police.

A drowsy voice said, "Sergeant's busy just now taking a statement."

With a stab of intuition, "Who from?"

The question was commanding and before he could collect himself the desk man said, "A Mr. and Mrs. Hughes."

And then in startled indignation, "Who are you, for the record?"

"Channon, Justin Channon."

"And I'm Robert E. Lee."

While officialdom adjusted its ego and its proud place, a mass of flesh, bone, and awakened fury might explode the kitchen door inwards, bolt or not.

"Tell the sergeant to come right out prepared for an arrest —possibly with violence—to Channon's farm. The charge is attempted murder. And tell him to hold Mrs. Hughes, and finish with her later. She's part of this, too."

L22   Finish? She must have arrived, in Bryn's hands, at some kind of dark end for herself, a lightless lifelong tunnel. But pay-back verbal finishing still had to be done on her part.

The other shoe in its final thump.

He hung up and leaned for a moment with his forehead pressed against the cool wall.

Clare beside him took back his hand. In an amazed strange voice, looking at the hand in hers, the grass-stained nails, she said, "I do, you know, and this is only a kind of telegram—that ghastly, that heap of a Ben Willett—I do thank God for you, Justin. Even though everything right now is so"—eyes enlarged, wide-seeing, on what was immediately to fall upon them, the sirens, the last bitter sediment of Meg—"so hopeless."

Justin had thought himself incapable for a while of any emotion whatever. He was wrong. A warmth stirred somewhere, a distant promising.

"Hopeless? No."

In this one case, the negative was an affirmative. He lifted the hand she had given him and kissed the back of it.

"Just," he said, "just, Clare, to be going on with."

Mary McMullen, who comes from a family of mystery writers, was awarded the Mystery Writers of America's Best First Mystery Award for her book *Strangle Hold*. Her other books include *Something of the Night, My Cousin Death, A Dangerous Funeral, But Nellie Was So Nice,* and *Welcome to the Grave.* She and her husband live in Albuquerque, New Mexico.